Praise for Tawny Weber

"*Double Dare* establishes Tawny Weber
as a new force in the Blaze lineup."
—*CataRomance*

"*Does She Dare?* is another sinfully spicy
and chocolate sweet read by the highly
entertaining and creative Tawny Weber."
—*Romance Junkies*

"A great setup, sizzling attraction and wonderful
characters all make *Risqué Business*,
by Tawny Weber, impossible to put down."
—*Romantic Times BOOKreviews*

"Tawny Weber weaves her magic with
Coming on Strong, another blazing-hot
tale of betrayal, love and passion....
With *Coming on Strong*, Tawny Weber will
quickly rise to the top of many auto buy lists."
—*CataRomance*

"They're wonderful! Totally sexy and romantic,
to boot! I know everyone will love them as
much as I do."
—Michelle Buonifiglio, *Romance B(u)y the Book*
on *Coming on Strong* and *Going Down Hard*

Dear Reader,

I had so much fun working with Sam, Karen and Lisa on this series, brainstorming all the ways a costume could open the door to so many secret fantasies. And I admit I went a little overboard with it. Because both my hero and heroine end up in disguise...and playing "what's-my-fantasy" is fantastic foreplay!

After spending her entire adult life avoiding her past, Zoe is forced to go back home in search of the one man who can save her brother's business. All she wants to do is get in, find the guy and get out with her dignity intact. When her costume turns out to be completely different than what she ordered, she ends up attending her high school reunion wearing leather and studs. Lucky for her, there's one guy who isn't intimidated at all by her dominatrix getup. In fact, he's begging for more....

I hope you enjoy Zoe and Dex's story. And I hope you'll join me in wishing Harlequin a very happy 60th Anniversary, as well as wishes for many more.

If you're on the Web, feel free to drop by my Web site at www.TawnyWeber.com and let me know what you think of Zoe and Dex's story. While you're there, check out my blog, vote for the hunk of the month, or enter my current contest. I'd love to hear from you.

Enjoy!

Tawny Weber

Tawny Weber

FEELS LIKE THE FIRST TIME

HARLEQUIN®

TORONTO • NEW YORK • LONDON
AMSTERDAM • PARIS • SYDNEY • HAMBURG
STOCKHOLM • ATHENS • TOKYO • MILAN • MADRID
PRAGUE • WARSAW • BUDAPEST • AUCKLAND

Recycling programs
for this product may
not exist in your area.

ISBN-13: 978-0-373-79496-6

FEELS LIKE THE FIRST TIME

Printed in U.S.A.

ABOUT THE AUTHOR

Tawny Weber is usually found dreaming up stories in her California home, surrounded by dogs, cats and kids. When she's not writing hot, spicy stories for Harlequin Blaze, she's testing her latest margarita recipe, shopping for the perfect pair of boots or drooling over Johnny Depp pictures (when her husband isn't looking, of course). When she's not doing any of that, she spends her time scrapbooking and playing in the garden. She'd love to hear from readers, so drop by her home on the Web, www.TawnyWeber.com.

Books by Tawny Weber

HARLEQUIN BLAZE

Don't miss any of our special offers. Write to us at the following address for information on our newest releases.

Harlequin Reader Service
U.S.: 3010 Walden Ave., P.O. Box 1325, Buffalo, NY 14269
Canadian: P.O. Box 609, Fort Erie, Ont. L2A 5X3

To Samantha Hunter, Karen Foley and
Lisa Renee Jones.

Ladies, this was a pleasure!

Prologue

SURROUNDED BY the makings of a million fantasies, Josie propped her chin on her fist and stared out the plate-glass window at her very own daydream—a hottie in a brown uniform, his name was Tom and he delivered thrills by the truckload. Of course, the thrills were actually costumes, and he didn't realize he was the star of all of her hottest dreams.

And at this rate, he never would.

"Another delivery for Dressed to Thrill," Tom said as he wheeled a loaded hand truck into the shop. "Hiya, Josie."

"Tom," she said softly, silently cursing her shyness. He was even cuter close-up. Wavy brown hair, bright-blue eyes and shoulders to die for. She always regretted September, since it meant he switched from shorts to long pants and covered those sexy legs.

Josie cast around for something clever to say, some conversation starter. But as always when she was around him, her mind went blank.

"How's business?" he asked as he stacked the boxes by the counter then handed her the electronic board to sign.

"Giving thrills is always good business," she responded automatically. His brown eyes widened. Josie realized what she said and blushed. Good thing her hands were full with the board and pen or she'd have slapped them over her mouth.

Then he grinned. "That's the store's tagline, isn't it? I've seen it on the labels. It must fit. This is definitely the place to go to make fantasies come true, huh?"

Conversation. Wow. *Don't drop the ball now,* she warned herself. Josie gave a hesitant smile back and nodded so fast, her blond bangs flew in her eyes. "Definitely. I'll show you."

Glad to finally have his interest as well as an excuse to keep him here a little longer, she grabbed a box opener and cut through the tape on the top carton.

"We get a lot of requests," she explained. "People want to live out their wildest desires, you know?"

She'd spent the past two months wondering what his desires were. Maybe now she'd find out?

Flipping back the tissue paper, she grabbed the first costume and pulled it out without looking. Her eyes were locked with Tom's, her mind giddy at finally having his attention.

"Can't you see how sexy this could be?" she asked. "Is it the kind of thing you might fantasize about?"

At the same time, they both glanced at the costume in her hands. A bunny rabbit. White, fluffy, sexless.

Josie's cheeks burned. She gripped the costume so tightly, she'd probably find fur under her fingernails.

Tom laughed and shook his head. "I don't know, Josie. I think bunnies have to be wearing bow ties to be considered sexy." With that and a friendly wave, he left. Just like that.

Josie managed to wait until the door closed before she groaned. As usual, she couldn't even manage a simple flirtation with the guy.

Of course, head-to-toe white fur didn't help matters.

"Definitely not fantasy material." She sighed and shook out the bunny costume before sliding it onto a hanger. "At least it wasn't a Smurf costume."

The next box of new costumes was better. A revealing slave-girl outfit, like something Princess Leia would have worn. A gorgeous cabaret getup. And, Josie sighed, a new Marilyn Monroe costume. All very sexy.

Unlike forest creatures and space aliens. She rolled her eyes. She'd blown it. What a dork, trying to flirt like that. She should have known better. She could no more flirt than she could just ask Tom out. Just imagining how bad she'd mess *that* up, her cheeks burned again in humiliation. But maybe she could drop a couple of hints next time he was in?

Contemplating different hints she could give without sounding stupid, Josie started to package costumes.

She glanced at the stack of Internet orders that needed to be shipped. A dominatrix for New York. A Betty Boop for Idaho. Sexy pirate in Pittsburgh. Gathering outfits for the already labeled boxes, she hummed a little tune. She frowned as she pulled the dominatrix costume from the rack. Could she ever find the nerve to wear something like this?

"Josie?"

She spun around, one hand still holding the other on her chest to calm her pounding heart.

"Tom?" She hoped he'd take her breathlessness as surprise instead of nerves. "What's up? I thought you'd already left."

He gave her a sheepish, little-boy grin that melted her insides. "I forgot to deliver one package."

He held out a small box. But he was staring at the costume in her hands. He eyed the skimpy leather, then shifted his gaze to Josie. Interest sparkled, a naughty smile quirking one corner of his mouth.

"Now that's an interesting getup," he said. "I don't suppose…"

Josie glanced at the leather in her hand, then back at Tom. Her eyes widened. Was he asking if she liked to play naughty? Color washed over her cheeks.

"The best thing about working at Dressed to Thrill is being able to role-play," she told him. Then she hesitated and with a deep breath said, "Like our slogan says, 'Bring us your fantasies, we'll make them come true.'"

Tom smiled, but before he could respond, the phone rang. With a shrug, he said, "We'd better get back to work. I'll see you tomorrow, okay?"

Josie didn't even pout when he left. Listening to her boss take the call, she grinned and gave a little dance and skip as she returned to the packing counter. He'd see her tomorrow. He'd said it like he was looking forward to it. Maybe tomorrow was the day he'd ask her out? Head filled with daydreams of Tom, she folded the dominatrix costume into the box heading for Idaho.

Wasn't love grand? She patted the black leather and smiled. She sure hoped this costume brought the wearer as much luck as it had brought her.

1

―――――

"THE GIRL VOTED most likely to die a virgin." "So unpopular, she attended her prom alone." "The queen of geek chic."

Zoe Gaston sneered at the labels people had scribbled under her senior picture. She hated labels. Although, she sighed as she glanced at the photo, sometimes it was hard to deny them. *An ode to the dark side,* she'd called her teen years. Black spiked hair, black-lined eyes, black glossy lips. She'd been a pudgy-cheeked brainy Goth-girl.

In other words, a total misfit.

"You think I should attend my ten-year reunion…why?" she asked Meghan with a grimace.

"To relive happy high-school memories and reconnect with all your friends, of course."

Zoe's sister-in-law actually believed that. She was the kind of gal who'd liked school. Plenty of friends, good times, general acceptance. The total opposite of Zoe's experience. Other than one brief weekend when the hottie football star she'd crushed on had seemed to return her interest, she'd spent her high-school years as persona non grata.

"Oh, yeah, the good ol' days." Zoe squinted at Meghan and nodded sagely. "That would be when the cheerleaders hated me, the jocks were terrified of me and the teachers, ah, yes, the teachers. They were just as happy when I cut class as when I showed up."

Meghan shrugged and snatched the yearbook away, obviously sensing the trip down memory lane wasn't helping her argument any. She tossed it on Zoe's electric-blue couch, the glossy cover swooshing across the slick leather.

"You publicly mocked the cheerleaders," she pointed out with a dirty look.

Oops. Zoe bit her lip to hold back a laugh as she realized perky Meghan probably had a pair of bronzed pom-poms hidden away somewhere.

"Zach told me you kicked the quarterback in the balls," Meghan continued, sounding shocked and irritated. Zoe raised her brow as if to ask what was wrong with that, but managed to keep her mouth shut as the other woman continued. "And he said you regularly argued with the teachers."

A quick grin escaped. Okay, so her school days hadn't totally sucked. "Exactly. I didn't fit in. I didn't want to fit in. And nobody wanted me to try to fit in. So why on earth would I go back?"

"To show them all how hot you are, how successful you are and how wrong they were about you."

"Sure. Because I still don't look like a Kewpie doll, I change jobs more often than most people change hairstyles and it's been so long since I had sex that I might as well be the lifelong virgin they dubbed me."

"So what? Those things don't mean they were right about you, do they? And it's not like you have to fill out some sexual-activity roster if you attend."

Zoe smirked, then picked up her margarita glass and took a sip. Before she could come up with a clever response,

Meghan puffed up her cheeks so she looked like an angry blond chipmunk, then blew out a gust of air. "If you don't go, they're all going to think they were right. Are you going to let them win?"

Zoe opened her mouth to say she didn't care if they won or not. Then she sighed and shut it again. She couldn't deny it. She *did* love to win. It was almost an irresistible need in her, that inability to step away from a competition, the compulsion to try to get the last word, to fight to the often-bitter end. It'd been the only thing that'd kept her in school after her parents' deaths—that need to prove all the gossips wrong.

Of course, as soon as the challenge was met and she'd won, she lost all interest. Boredom was Zoe's major downfall.

"I can overcome my need to win if I don't step up to play," she muttered, adding a silent *maybe*. She picked up the flashy neon invitation to the weeklong reunion and grimaced. "And returning to Central High's school of torture is good incentive to stay out of the game."

"And a rotten excuse for being afraid they might be right."

Zoe glared, but didn't respond to the direct hit.

"Why are you pushing this, really?" she asked, turning the tables. Zoe pointed to the bright reunion invitation that Meghan had brought over with an explanation that it'd been mailed to Zoe's brother when the committee hadn't been able to track her down. "You don't care if I relive my teen years or not, so what's behind it? The truth this time."

Meghan picked up a fuchsia pillow and ran her fingers through the fringe, her diamond wedding band sparkling. Finally, she looked up at Zoe with puppy-dog eyes and said, "Zach's in trouble."

Zoe sat upright so fast, her margarita sloshed over the edge of her glass. She ignored the icy stickiness trickling down her fingers and grabbed Meghan's arm. "What's wrong? What happened to Zach? Is he sick?"

"Nothing like that," Meghan hastened to assure her, her blue eyes wide and shocked at the vehement response. Zoe realized she might have overreacted a smidge, but Zach was all she had. "He's fine. Overworked and overstressed, as usual. It's not his health that's the problem. It's his business."

The fear slowly released its hold on her muscles. Zoe forced herself to breathe. Once, twice, then a deep, relieved sigh.

"Z-Tech?" she asked, referring to Zach's company. When the dot-com boom had gone belly-up, Zach had struck out on his own, creating a video-game company that catered to niche markets. Since she specialized in business consulting, Zoe had advised him more than once to expand his horizons, but Zach had always claimed he liked the cozy feel of specializing. He had decided last year to risk it all on his own platform. To compete with the likes of Sony and Microsoft, he'd gone with the concept of cheap, functional and expandable.

"Is his new system having problems?"

Meghan nodded. "He'd be furious if he knew I was telling you, but yeah. He sank everything, all our money, into this idea and now nobody is interested in the system. Not without something extra. If it doesn't take off, Z-Tech won't survive through the end of the year."

"Damn," Zoe breathed, sinking back in her chair.

Z-Tech was everything to Zach. Oh, sure, he adored his wife. But he'd loved that company first. He'd talked about starting it, had planned it way back when they were kids. Their parents had moved to Bradford, Idaho, when Zoe was fifteen. Zach, at eighteen, had stayed behind to try his luck in

Silicon Valley. When their parents had died, he'd set aside his dreams, moved to the small Idaho town to let Zoe finish high school and gone to work in the dot-com industry to support his sister.

Zach had given up everything for her. Zoe never forgot that. She owed him. Owed him for keeping her in school, for pushing her to excel instead of curling up in a ball of misery. Owed him for reminding her what family was, and what it meant to be loved when the whole world as she'd known it had turned into an upside-down hell. Not that he saw it that way. The few times she'd tried to express gratitude, he'd rolled his eyes and changed the subject.

Three years ago, after she'd quit yet another job, it'd been Zach who'd suggested Zoe pile all her qualifications into a portfolio and call herself a consultant. She could step in, boss people around, fix their problems, then leave before she got bored. Specializing in startups with growing pains, she evaluated, assessed and created business plans to help companies move to the next level. Or, a lot of times, to realize that they'd tapped out their market, in which case she pointed out options to reinvent themselves. It'd turned into the perfect—and very successful—solution to all of Zoe's career woes.

And now her brother, who'd essentially given her her career, was losing his own company. She set her glass on the side table with a frown. Nothing like the heavy taste of debt to ruin a perfectly good margarita.

"He had this idea, though," Meghan said, her tone hushed as though she was sharing secrets. "Zach was saying if he could get a hook, something special, he'd be able to make it work."

"Something to convince buyers to try his system? That they could only get with it?" Zoe clarified.

"Exactly."

"That's a great idea." Something Zoe had actually tried to suggest a few months back, but Zach had been in a weird macho   I-can-succeed-myself-and-prove-I'm-not-a-loser mood so it hadn't sunk in. If his business was in this bad shape, that probably accounted for his attitude, she realized now. What boredom was to her, failure was to her brother—pure hell. "What's the problem?"

"Zach figures he needs one killer game. An exclusive attached to his system. And there's only one game designer out there who's really exclusive, you know? Who everyone's heard of but who's never worked for one of the big companies."

Starting to see how this would circle back to her high-school reunion, Zoe waited.

"Apparently there's this guy. He goes by Gandalf the Gaming Wizard. He's the hottest video-game designer in the industry and he's a total mystery. Nobody knows who he really is. Zach's tried to reach him through Leeton, the company he works for, but no luck." Meghan got up with a bad-tempered "huff" and stalked to the large plate-glass window to stare out over the San Francisco skyline. "I tried to help Zach research him, but it's like digging in the dark. Nothing to go on but a few rumors."

Which was where the reunion issue came in. Zoe reached for her margarita glass and downed the rest of the watery contents. Oh, yeah, she'd heard plenty of rumors about Gandalf.

Meghan turned and, apparently seeing the recognition on Zoe's face, pointed in triumph. "You know him, don't you?"

"No." Not a lie. She had no idea who Gandalf was.

"But he knows you. He's got the hots for you. Even Zach admits it, although he growled a little bit when he did. It's obvious based on his launch game—Class Warfare."

"Circumstantial," Zoe dismissed, even though she knew Meghan was probably right. Five years ago, after hearing Zach rant about it, she'd checked the game out herself. The designer had obviously lived in Bradford at some point. The similarities were glaring: landmarks, sayings, class slogans. Her.

She gave a little shiver. She'd never been able to pinpoint if she was flattered or freaked that the main character, a busty heroine named SweetCheeks, had been based on her. Not so much in looks—or bra size—but in attitude. Some of her catchphrases, her habit of tapping her lip when she was thinking. The purple-tipped, spiked black hair she'd sported in school. And more specifically, the one-of-a-kind tribal wings tattoo on her shoulder blades Zoe had gotten at sixteen in memory of her mother.

It was like a strange homage to her teenage self. A nice antidote to the ignominy of being voted most likely to die a virgin. The guy obviously knew her. But him? As far as she knew, nobody had a clue who he was.

"Circumstantial my ass," Meghan returned, slapping her hands on her denim-clad hips and glaring. "The answer to Zach's prayers, the hottest video-game designer in the country, is from your town. And chances are, given that he knew you in school well enough to see your naked back, he's likely your age. So he'd be at this reunion. Doh…it's a connect-the-dots win. Even you can focus long enough to connect dots, can't you?"

"Nobody likes a smart-ass," Zoe muttered, her lips twitching as she uttered the lie.

"Sure they do," Meghan claimed, sensing Zoe wasn't going to slam the door on the discussion. "Zach and I love you."

The trickle of guilt intensified.

Needing to move, Zoe got up and crossed the apartment to the kitchen. A push of the button on the blender whirred a nice loud distraction, as well as mixing up another batch of margaritas.

Central High. Cliquish, snotty and judgmental. Zoe had never fitted in. She'd been an odd dichotomy. A moody fifteen-year-old Goth-girl brainiac with a chip on her shoulder. She'd taken to the exclusive small town and its high school like a cat to water. Thankfully she'd had Dex. Because of him, her one friend, she'd been able to ignore how poorly she'd been accepted. Until she was sixteen and her parents had died in a car accident and she'd had to deal with another nasty small-town reality. Gossip. While she'd been trying to deal with her shock and grief, the gossip mill had gone into overtime, whispering on every corner rumors of her parents' pending divorce and claiming it was over her mom having an affair with the school principal.

Zoe had wanted to drop out, go anywhere and hide. But Zach had insisted she graduate. He'd set aside his dreams to be responsible. Despite the rotten high-school experience, she was grateful that he hadn't let her wienie out. Wasn't it her job, now, to set aside her irritation with the past to give *his* dreams a chance? After all, she wanted him to succeed, And even more, she wanted to prove herself. To him. And to herself.

Zoe sighed. Talk about pressure. She carried the pitcher into the living room and refilled both glasses.

"You know he'd be pissed if he found out you were doing this," she muttered to her sister-in-law as she sat back down. But she still picked up the invitation. "Nobody's even sure if Gandalf is from Bradford. You know that, right? He could have just passed through. There's no real reason to believe he's going to be at the reunion."

"Zach thinks he will be. Anyone that sentimental about his hometown would go to his reunion. The timing, a bunch of things in the game, suggest he's your age. Zach's been racking his brain to figure out a way to find the guy."

The guilt was a waterfall now.

Seeing the crack in Zoe's armor, Meghan moved in for the kill. She gave a perky smile and tugged a fat envelope out of her purse. "Look, here's more information on the reunion. I found the link when I used that Web site, you know? The Classmates one? When I saw your class was having a reunion, I e-mailed them to send me the invitation package."

Zoe's eyebrow arched. So that's how they'd really found her. She'd wondered. It wasn't like she'd left a trail of bread-crumbs for her ex-schoolmates to track her down.

"There was even speculation about Gandalf there on the message boards," Meghan continued, once she was sure Zoe wasn't going to chide her for the behind-the-back maneuvering. "People wondering if he's really from your school. What class he was in. If he'll come to the reunion. That kind of thing."

Figured. More gossip, this time cyber-style. Zoe just rolled her eyes.

"Even if he is there, it's not like he's going to be wearing a sign. The guy's managed to keep his identity a secret from major competitors for five years. He won't show up wearing a pointed hat and carrying a game controller." Seeing the stubborn look on Meghan's face, Zoe sighed. Then, as she did when faced with any impossible business challenge, she started breaking it down into smaller tasks to research, areas to consider, things to do. In other words, her brain had gone into strategy mode.

While she mulled all the angles, she absently took the reunion booklet Meghan held out. When she flipped the neon cover open, all thoughts of strategy fled; Zoe's stomach knotted. With narrowed eyes, she looked at the grainy black-and-white picture of the king and queen. Brad Young and Candice Love. Her crush and the girl who'd stolen him away from her.

She gave a low growl. Candice was the mean, snotty bitch behind making Zoe's high-school life a living hell. Galaxies apart socially, the two girls had been in direct competition in most things academic. Zoe snickered, remembering that four out of five times, she'd beaten Candice.

But Candice had had her revenge. Her whispers had taken Zoe's one spark of happiness and turned it into a worthless misery. Buzz of Zoe's parents and the affair had surfaced the same week she'd won the Governors' Award for Excellence. Candice had been the one whispering loudest, saying that since Zoe's mom had been fooling around with the principal, his recommendation and support of Zoe were based on her mother's bedroom skills. Zoe hadn't believed the gossip. She knew her parents were having problems, but cheating wasn't one of them. But she'd never forgiven Candice for starting the ugly rumor. Or for planting those doubts in Zoe's head.

Which meant helping out her brother was also her chance to go back, show the stuck-up cheerleader and her gang of friends that she was all those things Meghan tried to convince her she was. Hot and successful.

"Okay, fine," she decided with a determined thrust of her chin. "I'll go."

"Thanks, Zoe." Meghan's gratitude, apparent in her blue eyes and huge, relieved smile, gave Zoe a warm feeling. Helping was good. Meghan picked up the reunion folder and flipped through the pages. "You need a costume. And you're late sending an RSVP, so it might be hard to get a room at the reunion hotel."

"I'm going, but I'm not wearing some stupid costume. The last thing I want to do is dress up and make nice with the people who so easily judged and dismissed me," she sneered as though she didn't care. And she didn't. At least, not much.

"Please, Zoe. If you're going to get these people to help you find Gandalf, you have to at least pretend you're going to play their game."

Zoe wrinkled her nose. Play nice? She hadn't factored that into her calculations. But the pitiful begging look on Meghan's face forced her to nod.

"I'll take care of the RSVP," she said with her best negotiation smile. "The reunion is at Drake Inn. I know the owners. So I'll be right there in the thick of things and able to track down all the Gandalf insider info. But I'm not doing a costume."

Meghan waved the purple and orange flyer. "You have to. It's a *costume* party!" she declared.

"No, thanks," Zoe said. "I'll find a sexy little dress and wear that instead."

She wasn't going for the reunion festivities. She was going to help out her brother. And maybe, just maybe for a second shot at the crush that got away. A chance to show the hottie football star, Brad Young, just what he'd missed out on. Blond and buff, he'd inspired many a fantasy and her sadly failed attempt to divest herself of that pesky virginity problem.

And then he'd left her high and dry.

Oh, yeah. The promise of showing everyone—Brad, Candice and all the people who'd mocked her—just how well she was doing was the last bit of incentive she needed to return to hell and chase down Gandalf.

As she imagined that scenario and considered shopping for new lingerie, Zoe tapped her bottom lip and considered. Die a virgin, her ass. The problem with a title like that, though, was how the hell did one prove it wrong?

Two weeks later

ZOE STRODE UP TO the beveled-glass doors of the Drake Inn, her four-inch stiletto boots rat-a-tat-tatting against the stamped cement. She'd spent a lot of time here in her teens since her best friend Dex's parents owned the place.

After Meghan had convinced her to attend the reunion, Zoe had pulled out her one photo album and laughed over the few happy memories she had of Bradford. All of them had included her best friend, Dex.

As much an oddball as she was, Dex had joined in with Zoe's schemes and dreams. They had sketched castles in the air of the wonders they'd accomplish when they were out from under the oppressive judgment of all the small-town minds that didn't understand them.

A brainy Goth-girl and a geeky math nerd, both proud not to fit in with their mainstream classmates.

She could use some of that youthful arrogance now. Oh, sure, she was still distinctive and self-assured. People treated her with respect, curried her favor and sought out her professional advice. But as soon as she drove into town, all her old doubts, self-consciousness and worry about not fitting in had hit her.

It'd been one thing to plan a brilliant reunion coup with Meghan in her living room, to draw up a list of ideas, just the way she'd outline a plan of attack for one of the flailing businesses that regularly consulted her. Zoe had made a roster of people to talk to. She'd gone through the yearbook and researched all of her classmates, coming up with a list of possible wizards. She'd e-mailed everyone she knew in the business industry who might have any ideas about Gandalf, and she had had Meghan use Zach's contacts to dig for information.

Her plan for this week? Divide and conquer. She'd talk to everyone on her list, from teacher to geek. She'd poke around all the places Gandalf featured in his video games and see if she could find some clues. She'd pull strings, make nice and play sleuth. One way or another, if Gandalf was in Bradford, Zoe would track him down for Zach.

But now, faced with actually implementing the plan? She remembered what it'd felt like to be a gawky teen. Only now she didn't have her Gothic F-you attitude to hide behind. Of course, she'd been faking it ten years ago anyway.

She squared her shoulders. It'd served her well enough before, so she might as well fake it again. Phony attitude or not, she was on a mission. Like SweetCheeks, she had her orders and she was here to kick ass.

Snickering at the image, Zoe reached the door and paused. She really didn't want to go in there. The only way this could be less appealing was if she was going in for a back-to-back mammogram, root canal, public weigh-in.

Would anyone recognize her? Maybe she wasn't a pudgy Goth dressed in black with spiked hair and random piercings, but, as she glanced at her reflection in the door, she realized she hadn't changed *that* much. Her short, wild hair was still black in places, along with chunky red and blond highlights. She still sported an extra five pounds, but now she emphasized those curves instead of hiding them in baggy T-shirts. And while she'd let most of her piercings close up, she wore a small diamond in her nose and eight in each ear.

Yeah, she was still "different." But at least now, she had

enough confidence in her abilities not to let that bother her. Unlike in high school, when she'd been stuck in this town with no options, for this round she'd come with an agenda. And that gave her the advantage. She was on the ball and in command.

And flying monkeys were delivering her luggage.

Amused by her own idiotic pep talk, Zoe grabbed the brass handle and swung the door open.

Showtime.

Ten minutes and a room key later, Zoe crossed the lobby, congratulating herself. She'd checked in, gotten her reunion welcome package and managed to avoid any actual reunions.

"Zoe? Zoe Gaston, the chic geek?"

The shrill chorus stopped her in her tracks. Zoe gave a horrified little spasm before clearing her face and turning toward the giggling.

The Fenton sisters. Two perfect, redheaded porcelain dolls with hearts of ice. Zoe had to fight to put a fake smile on her face. She fought even harder against the urge to run.

"Hello," she voiced tonelessly. "Fancy seeing you here."

"Well, well. You've certainly changed," one said. The other eyed her up and down, probably gauging the cost of her outfit— skinny jeans, ankle boots and a black velvet tunic—to the nearest dollar and, from her sneer, figuring she'd overpaid.

"Amazing, isn't it?" Zoe shot back with a smirk of her own. "And yet, neither of you have at all."

Julie and Jackie, or Jingle and Jangle as Zoe had dubbed them in school due to their shrill voices and her lack of ability to tell them apart, engulfed her in perfume-laced hugs. Just as oblivious as she remembered, they didn't even notice her stiff-as-a-board lack of a reaction. They just launched into a babbling cacophony of chatter and gossip. As though she was one of them.

Zoe's eyes narrowed. The twins had never had time for her ten years ago. She'd have sworn that if it weren't for Candice's sour-grapes gossip-fest over the award, they wouldn't have even known her name. And now they were welcoming her and acting like she was their friend?

What were they up to?

"Did you hear Brad Young is here? He's divorced now, I heard. And still the hottest thing ever, but now he's rolling in the dough." Jangle tittered.

It was all Zoe could do not to look around in case Brad was actually here in the lobby. How had he aged? Did he remember her? More important, did he remember their one and only date? The one he'd cut short for no reason, mid makeout session. The one that had broke her teenaged heart and leveled her tentative faith in the acceptance of her peers.

Zoe shook off the irritating memories and the doubts they dredged up and focused on the twins' speculation about how Brad, who'd needed that football scholarship to go to college, had struck it rich. Jingle shot Zoe a snide look, her smile dripping glee. "Remember that crazy rumor about you and Brad at the drive-in?"

Had they read her thoughts? Zoe narrowed her eyes, glad that she'd never been the blushing type. The redheads' giggle made it clear just how unbelievable they thought the idea of Zoe and the captain of the football team doing the movie mambo was. The speculative look, the disdain in their cornflower-blue eyes, confirmed Zoe's suspicion. They weren't welcoming her as an old classmate. They were priming her for fodder.

She sighed. Figured. In school, they'd been the gossip

queens. Nothing happened but they got the first dirt on it. Obviously they were reprising their grimy roles all over again.

Zoe ground her teeth to keep from telling them to mind their own business. She knew this gossip game was her best shot at tracking down clues on Gandalf. If she wanted to win, she had to play. She considered a coquettish giggle of her own but figured she'd choke on it. Instead, she arched one brow and gave a naughty smile.

Lashes fluttering like stiff caterpillars, two sets of heavily lined eyes widened and the women stepped closer.

"Hey, I'm not a kiss-and-tell kind of gal," she said. The twins exchanged shocked looks. Perfect. Maybe they'd be willing to barter for information on who might be the gaming wizard. From her research, four of the guys in the graduating class were possibilities. Much to her dismay, one of them happened to be Brad, who'd gone on to be a computer-science major.

Zoe hoped that a little gossip-gathering, some more online research once she got her hands on the attendee bios at the reunion welcome party tonight, and she'd have all the info she needed to pinpoint Gandalf. But she couldn't deny the thought of facing Brad put her on edge.

"Of course, I'm sure nobody's interested in my little secrets," she said, launching the gossip-gathering portion of her plan. "After all, I'm not one of the graduating class to go on to fame and fortune. I've heard quite a few did, though. C'mon, all the former classmates' lives can't be complete secrets. Don't we know what a few people are doing? You know, like who's married to who, where everyone is living? Or who's hit it big?"

"Well," one of the sisters said, exchanging a look with the other, "we do have a few details, of course. I mean, keeping up with what everyone's been doing is sort of a hobby of ours."

"Do tell," Zoe encouraged while mentally mocking her vapid performance.

"Well," said one of them, leaning closer. "Do you remember Teresa Roberts? She was that girl who had such a big crush on you?" She barely waited for Zoe's wince before continuing, "She's filthy rich, I hear. Huge success in writing computer programs of some kind."

Teresa? Computer success? But Gandalf was a guy, wasn't he? Then again, this was Teresa. The only person in high school other than Brad to ever show any semblance of interest in Zoe. Maybe using a guy's name wasn't so far-fetched.

Before she could ask for details, another woman Zoe didn't recognize joined them in a chorus of squeals and giggles.

Zoe winced. She'd dig for more gossip later, hopefully without having to hear any more shrill laughter. Before she could break in and excuse herself, a ruckus across the room caught her attention.

Someone had overturned a full luggage cart. The giggle twins still babbling in her ear, Zoe watched a guy hurry forward to help collect the bags. Something tugged in the back of her mind, but she ignored it in favor of watching the delicious view as he bent low to retrieve the scattered suitcases.

There it was. The finest ass she'd ever seen. Nerves fluttered in her throat and she tapped her finger against her bottom lip as she considered the odds of the front equaling the back. Long shot, she knew. Guys were either good to watch coming or going.

And it'd been a long cold spell since she'd seen a guy coming.

The man straightened, the luggage all reloaded on the cart and the embarrassed guest reassured. He turned toward Zoe and stopped as if he'd hit a glass wall. Their gazes met. She felt the impact all the way across the room. Her tummy spiraling like she'd fallen off a cliff, Zoe's breath caught. Her body went from hot to blazing.

Gorgeous, was all she could think.

Shaggy coffee-brown hair was shoved off a face that made her think of poets and scholars. His long jawline and dark brows gave intensity to a face that would be pretty otherwise. She wanted, needed, to see his eyes. Were they as sexy close-up as they seemed from across the room?

A loose, blue button-up covered broad shoulders but hid his arms and chest. Zoe wondered what that chest was like. Was he muscled and hard? Or soft and snuggly? Her eyes skimmed the shirt fabric and dropped to the well-fitted denim hugging his slender hips. She sighed in appreciation as she noted how the worn fabric hinted that he dressed left. It was all she could do not to walk over and cup that fabric herself and confirm the suspicion.

Yeah, his body pretty much screamed sex to her. Hot, unbridled, mind-blowing-orgasm sex.

He smiled at her. A crooked, sexy smile that rang a bell in the back of her head. But she was too busy paying attention to the sirens going off in her body to pay attention to it.

His smile pulled her in. She automatically smiled back. Just as automatic was the shoulders-back-breasts-high shift as she angled her body toward him. Suddenly she had a second agenda besides snagging Gandalf this week—to see how many ways she could see this guy come.

2

DEXTER DRAKE FROZE as his gaze met Zoe's across the room. Even from ten yards away, he could see the sparkle in her eyes. If eyes were the windows to the soul, Zoe's were clear plate glass. Everything she felt was reflected in those bottle-green depths. And right now the reflection was an interesting mix of irritation and intrigue. He'd like to think the intrigue was a little sexual, a hint of interest in him. But even though he'd made a fortune with his imagination, Dex wasn't the kind of guy who lied to himself.

More likely, she was trying to figure out why the hell, at his age, he was apparently still working at his parents' hotel. Dex winced. This wasn't how he'd planned to greet her for the first time. He'd hoped to make it a surprise. Preferably when she was alone instead of surrounded by a gaggle of giggling women who reminded him of overaged teenagers. Maybe when he was dressed decently, and not, he grimaced with a glance at his jeans, like one of those overaged teens himself.

Regardless of timing, Dex couldn't stop his grin. All he'd been able to think about for the past couple weeks was seeing Zoe again. And there she was. While he'd have recognized her trademark dimple and sassy head tilt anywhere, the rest of her was a delicious surprise.

Sleek and sexy, she wasn't Goth anymore, but her rebellious individuality was still apparent. No longer short, spiky and pitch-black, her hair hit her shoulders in a cacophony of curls and chunky streaks of color. Red, blond and, yeah, he was happy to see, still some black. She'd lost the roundness that ten years ago she'd lamented and he'd secretly loved. Her black top fell in a straight line to her thighs, but didn't disguise the swell of her breasts or the indention of her waist. A stack of thick silver bangles clanged on her wrist every time she moved her arm, matching metal glinting from her ears.

Just as Dex raised his hand to wave to her, she gave him one last, long glance. Then she turned away. He frowned. What was up with that? He caught his own reflection in the large mirror behind the registration desk and realized that as much as she'd changed, so had he.

Ten years ago, he'd been a foot shorter, built like a noodle and worn glasses. Laser eye surgery, a good workout program and the discovery of protein had definitely had their effects on his body.

Cool. He could still surprise her. With that in mind, Dex worked his way around the lobby. He positioned himself between the clucking clutch of women and Zoe's probable escape route so he could step out and greet her once she headed for her room. He kicked back against one of the rosewood columns, crossed his ankles and arms and let loose a grin. He couldn't wait to see the look on her face when she saw him.

A year younger that Zoe, Dex had taken a lot of advanced classes with her. Brainiacs like them tended to band together. But she'd never seen him as more than a sidekick. A younger buddy. Funny, safe and sexless. Emasculating, yes, but still better than the rest of his schoolmates, who usually saw him only as a wallet or the keys to the best party house in town.

After Zoe had graduated and left town, Dex had lost all interest in Central High and had counted the days until his own graduation. A scholarship to MIT had been his ticket away from the memories of his unrequited crush and out from under his father's ever-unfulfilled demands. College, life and a little bit of luck had healed his bruised heart. But he'd never forgotten Zoe. And now was his chance to reconnect, hopefully on equal footing this round.

He heard one of the ditzy chicks ask, "So, who are you looking forward to seeing again, Zoe?"

His ears, among other things, perked up. He'd love to hear her say his name. Crazy wish, since he wasn't even a member of her graduating class and she'd have no reason to expect him here. But the seventeen-year-old in his heart still wished just a little.

"Oh, you know, everyone," Zoe hedged. Dex snickered. He knew better than anyone what a lie that was. They'd spent hours on end holed up here at the hotel, raiding the kitchen and lamenting the nastiness of their peers.

"C'mon, there must be someone you're looking forward to seeing again," one of the women nudged. "Maybe Brad?"

Dex shot upright, peering around the column to frown at Zoe's face. Brad? Brad Young? That ass? With an ugly surge of jealousy, Dex remembered Zoe's crush on the blond jock. Unlike the typical jock, Brad hadn't been an idiot. Just a jerk. He and Dex had gone head to head in all things science. And usually, Dex remembered with a snicker, he'd won.

"Maybe," Zoe said with a shrug. Resentment momentarily forgotten, Dex watched the way the soft black fabric of her top moved. Touchably soft, the material emphasized her round breasts. He'd spent years dreaming about those breasts. Lusting as only a callow, teenage boy could. And she'd been lusting after Brad the cad.

Dex ground his teeth. If her questions were anything to go by, she still was.

"Actually, it sounds like Brad's done really well for himself," she said in the offhand tone that people used to pretend they don't care. "But Julie mentioned nobody's sure how. Sounds like a mystery. Anybody have a clue?"

She asked the question with the enthusiasm and verve that'd always inspired him to crazy acts. Like TPing the science hall, letting the air out of the tires of the entire track team's vehicles and rigging the microphones so everybody on the debate team had sounded like Donald Duck.

"I hear it was the stock market. He pulled out just before Wall Street tanked last year," one of the redheads said.

"Are you sure?" the one who looked just like her asked. "I heard he's doing something creative with his degree in computer science. Writing or something like that."

"No, no, no," interrupted the third woman. "He inherited a pile of money from his great-granddad."

The three women compared gossip sources while Zoe watched, transfixed, as if the answer to Brad's success meant world peace and calorie-free chocolate.

Dex shoved his fists in his pockets and kicked at the pillar. After all these years, all the crap the guy had done to her, she still wanted to see Brad? Didn't she ever learn?

Hell, didn't he? When his mom had told him Zoe's class was holding its reunion at the hotel, he'd been intrigued. When she'd mentioned Zoe had booked a room, he hadn't been able to resist a trip home. Even if it meant facing his dad's nagging that, instead of starting his own business, he invest all his savings in the Drake, and his mom's lamenting that he was ruining his life by quitting his well-paying job as a video-game designer and going out on his own. Using one of his hard-learned lessons from high school, he'd dealt with their negativity by throwing money toward a fancy vacation for them and sending them packing with the assurance that he'd take care of the hotel while they were away.

Anything for a chance to hang out with his best friend again. And yeah, he admitted to himself, a chance to nurture that tiny hope that he and Zoe might be a little more than friends this time. He imagined the two of them, cuddled up in the tree house back behind the inn property where they'd planned so many teenage escapades. In his imagination, Zoe's sweet body was naked as she poised over him calling him big boy and urging him to new heights of pleasure.

Who said you couldn't go back in time? Dex grinned. Five minutes in her presence and he was already fantasizing like a seventeen-year-old again.

"I was surprised that careers and bios weren't listed in the reunion program," Zoe said, pulling his attention back to the giggling group. "I mean, isn't everyone here to catch up on what everyone else has done? I'd think Brad's success would be the talk of the reunion."

His hope—among other things—shriveled at her words.

"I'm on the reunion committee," the blond lady said importantly. "We wanted to make this fun, involve everyone in a game or two. You know, like 'guess the careers.' That's why we decided to kick things off tonight with the costume party. It's all a part of the theme. Didn't you read your welcome package? You're supposed to give hints, but keep your actual career a secret. On Wednesday, we'll play the match game and everyone can share then."

"Lovely," Zoe said tonelessly, her smile strained. "Was that supposed to tie in somehow to our costume? The whole career angle?"

"Well, yeah," blondie said with a roll of her eyes. "But it's supposed to be, you know, like a riddle. Not a giveaway."

From Zoe's infinitesimal grimace, her riddle was going to be figuring out how to turn whatever costume she had into a tie-in to her job. Dex couldn't wait to find out what she'd ended up doing. He'd tried checking up on her a few times over the years, but he'd never had much luck. She didn't even have a Facebook page. It baffled the mind.

"I'll bet Candy Love is coming as some kind of super-woman. She's just so perfect, isn't she? I can't wait to hear what she's been up to," said one of the redheads.

The look on Zoe's face was priceless. If he remembered correctly, and when it came to Zoe he usually did, she'd hated Candice. With good reason. Like Brad and him, the two girls had gone head to head in all things academic, with Zoe walking away with the lion's share of the winnings.

"I guess I'll see you all later," was all she said though. "It was a long flight and I'm a little tired. I might just skip the costume party and catch up with everyone tomorrow."

"Oh, no," chorused the ex-cheerleaders in perfect harmony. They all giggled, then one of the redheads said, "You have to come to the welcome bash. After all, Brad will be there."

Zoe's drooping shoulders straightened at that and she tapped her hip as though she was weighing her choices. Then she shrugged and said, "Sure. I'll see you all there." She shifted her purse and prepared to leave, then hesitated and said, "If you see Brad, tell him I'd like to talk to him, okay?"

She headed across the lobby away from the pillar Dex was hiding behind. Frowning, he watched the sway of her hips as she departed, not bothering to follow her.

Brad Young. Again.

Dex shoved his hands into the front pockets of his jeans with a silent growl. He'd be damned if he'd waste his last week of vacation watching the woman he'd come across the country to see fall all over some other guy. Especially not his old nemesis. Damned if he was going to spend the week taking a backseat in Zoe's attention to that jerk the way he had all through school.

Not that he figured he had a claim on Zoe. Hell, it'd been ten years and he knew she'd never seen him as anything but a buddy. Sure, he'd had a few fantasies of changing her viewpoint, but they didn't even know each other anymore. And the last thing he needed at this juncture of his life was to hook himself into a relationship. So no, no matter what his analytical brain tried to label it, this was not jealousy.

Brad Young was a dick. A class-A jerk who'd always been out for himself. Oh, sure, he'd always made it look like he was Mr. Friendly. Despite their scholastic competitions, he'd gone out of his way to make friends with Dex, had invited him to hang out. Only the hanging out was always at the Drake's rec room and Dex was always the one footing the bill. When Dex had wised up and called him on it, Brad had denied that was why he'd kept him around. But when Dex's wallet had closed, the invites had ended.

What really pissed Dex off, though, was that Brad had used Zoe. Things like getting her to write his papers, pretending to be her friend while mocking her behind her back. He'd even tagged her with the lousy moniker of longest-living virgin or something like that. All because he'd lost a bet with his football pals about getting down her pants at the drive-in.

Dex didn't figure an asshole like that changed much over time. So it was up to him to protect his old friend. For all her tough shell, Zoe was sensitive. He'd have to make sure she wasn't used or hurt this week.

Yeah. That was it. It was for her own good that he'd be doing his damndest to monopolize her time and keep her away from Brad. Definitely nothing to do with jealousy.

As he settled that lie in his head, the twins sauntered past, hips swaying as they whispered together. One of them caught sight of him and stopped, lifted a brow and gave him a long, slow once-over.

"Well, hello. Are you here for the reunion?" she asked in a throaty purr.

"Nah," Dex said, a little unnerved to realize what the phrase *eat him up with her eyes* actually felt like. It made him want to put protective hands over his privates. "Wrong year."

"Too bad. Maybe we can talk about new times instead of old, then," she murmured before letting her sister tug her away.

Call him a wimp, but it was all he could do not to run.

"Dexter."

And there was a voice that never inspired the urge to escape. With a reluctant grin, he turned to face the elderly woman.

"Nana, I thought you were fleecing Vegas of its riches," he said as he bent in half to hug his tiny grandmother. The frailty under his hands was an illusion, he knew. Essie Drake was the strongest woman in the world.

"Vegas was rigged," she said with a sniff. Still in her travel wear—a tracksuit of some fuzzy red fabric—her white hair in curls and her gold-rimmed bifocals, she should have looked like Mrs. Claus. Except she was too small, skinny and if Dex were honest, naughty, to be that sainted lady. Instead, Nana looked like a mischievous elf who'd put saltpeter in Santa's cocoa and graffiti the sleigh.

She was his favorite person. His absolute champion. And the biggest pain in his butt. But any irritation was worth having her in his corner.

His parents had never understood his fascination with video games. They'd always figured it was a bad habit he'd outgrow. They'd been thrilled that he'd gone to college. Although his father said he'd only ponied up the funds for Dex's college expenses so that his son could earn big money and support the family business after graduation. That those expenses had been trivial considering Dex had a full-ride scholarship didn't negate the expectation in the slightest. No surprise that when, eight years ago, he'd decided to drop out of college and pursue his passion, his parents had thrown a fit.

But Nana? She'd cheered and urged him to strike out on his own. Her faith and encouragement supporting him, he'd combined graphic-design skills he'd learned in school, his computer obsession and the vivid imagination he'd always hidden for fear of being teased. The results, a highly successful career as a video-game designer. As a nod to his father's worries—and his own self-consciousness at sharing his creative side—Dex had designed under a pseudonym, since his first game had featured—and mocked—the small Idaho town that his father's ancestors had founded. Because of his discretion, and his Nana's unwavering championship, his parents had eventually tolerated his career choice enough to let him come home for the holidays. The buckets of money he'd made hadn't hurt either. Funny how money had a way of paving the way with people. All his life, the impression of money had opened doors. Friends, invitations, opportunities to hang with the in crowd.

Only Zoe hadn't cared about what he had. She'd simply accepted him for himself, not for what she could get out of him. Which brought the number of people who did to a grand total of two. Zoe and Nana.

"Is your sweetie here yet?" his grandmother asked, looking around the lobby. "Did I miss her?"

"Is that why you're back early? Another matchmaking game? Look, Nana, I don't have a sweetie. I'm just here to help out Mom and Dad before I get too busy."

Nana shook her head, a look of censure in her bright-blue eyes. "Dexter, I have the sight. I see you and your sweetheart hooking up soon."

Dex's jaw dropped. "Hooking up? Where do you come up with these things?"

He skipped right over the "sight" comment. Nana thought she was psychic. She claimed to have precognitive dreams and carried around a tarot deck. Much to his parents' chagrin, she liked to set up a table in the hotel lobby and offer readings to gullible guests. Recently Nana had taken her dreams on the road, attempting to supplement her retirement income by hitting the jackpot. So far, she'd had three trips to Vegas and five to Reno, and the most she'd won was a huge stuffed monkey dressed like Liberace.

"Admit it, you're here to find your one true love," his grandmother nagged, tucking her hand around his arm so he could lead her out the back door toward her cottage in the private grounds.

Zoe's image popped into his mind. But it wasn't love his imagination was interested in, given that she was naked and spread out over his bed.

"No true love, Nana. I don't have time." Or more to the point, love didn't have time for him. Dex had tried to fall in love, he'd really wanted to believe in the sweet myth of un-conditional emotions. But love, like his childhood, had always come with a price: money, favors, connections.

Nana sniffed and stuck out her narrow chin. "Love doesn't happen on a schedule, you know. You'd do well to find her this week, before you risk everything in this crazy scheme of yours."

"I thought you liked gambling," was all he said. He'd heard all the reasons his family didn't want him to go through with his plans. Four generations of Drakes had run this hotel and it was now on his shoulders to keep it in the family. His par-ents would tolerate him not directly working in the building, but family tradition demanded that he help keep the business afloat in these hard economic times. *Blah blah blah.*

But when this vacation ended next Monday, he'd make the biggest change of his adult life. He was leaving his well-paying job at Leeton Games and putting all his resources toward starting his own company. Years of dreaming, months of planning, and it was time to make his move. A familiar mantle of nerves settled on his shoulders and Dex tried to shrug it off. After all, the money didn't worry him much. Nor did the risk, even though it was a huge one given that the guy who'd drawn up his business plan and who was supposed to sign on as his manager had backed out, citing worries over having to start a company without being able to use Dex's main claim to fame. His pseudonym.

But Dex had an agreement with Leeton Games. When he'd

started there, the pseudonym had been his idea, but the notoriety it had built over the years had garnered the company a lot of accolades. In return for relinquishing all claims to the name and keeping silent for three years, they'd pay him enough money to give him a healthy cushion for a year to get his business going.

Dex had enough faith in his skills, his talents, to know that the computer-graphics company would take off.

But it was a damned shame his alter ego, Gandalf, had to be thrown on to the sacrificial pyre in the name of insurance.

"DID YOU FIND Gandalf yet?" Meghan asked over the speakerphone. Her words were impatient, her tone the equivalent of an irritated shove in the small of Zoe's back.

Zoe paused in the act of unpacking to shake her head at the phone. "I've been here an hour, Meg. It's not like the guy is going to be wearing a sign or anything. The biggest companies in video gaming have tried to find his identity for years now and failed. But you think all I have to do is saunter into the hotel and poof, there he'll be? I'm good, but not quite that good."

"If anyone can do it, you can," Meghan insisted. "But you have to talk to people. You know that, right? Did you ask around or did you register then beeline to your room to hide?"

"I talked, I asked. I'm trying, okay?" Zoe's irritated tone was in strong contrast to the underlying panic in her sister-in-law's voice. Zoe sucked in a breath and tried for calm. "Don't stress so much, okay? If the guy is here, I'll find out." Zoe recalled the twin's assertion about Teresa Roberts, but dismissed the idea. Gandalf had to be a guy.

"What's your first step? What're you doing tonight?"

Zoe winced. She'd been hoping Meghan wouldn't ask that.

She hated I-told-you-so moments. Hoping to avoid this one, she talked fast. "I figured I'd hang out in my room tonight. You know, do a little online research, touch base with a few people in the industry and see if they have any leads. And I still need to figure out how to convince this guy to work for Zach once we find him. I've got a few ideas, but I need to polish them before I run them by Zach since it's his company and money."

"No," Meghan broke in. "Wait to talk to Zach until you've found Gandalf."

Zoe snickered. "Hiding this little venture, are we?"

Meghan's huff blew through the phone, making Zoe laugh out loud. "Why aren't you attending the reunion's costume party tonight?" Meghan asked. That shut up Zoe's laughter.

"You were right," she admitted with a sigh. "Costumes are mandatory to attend the event. Dressing up in a costume that represents your career is part of the whole reunion game plan. They've created all these events during the week to force people to get to know each other again." Zoe kept her *As if I care to* to herself, figuring Meghan would launch into her lecture again.

"You need to go."

"No, I don't," Zoe argued, figuring Meghan would pitch the idea of her going in her pajamas if she left even the tiniest opening for argument.

"You do. You have to. This is the perfect way to eliminate the reunion members from your search. Just check out their costumes, right? So you have to go. And to make sure you do, I took care of everything," Meghan said in a bossy yet begging sort of tone that pushed all Zoe's guilt buttons. "I ordered you a costume. It should be delivered any time."

With a sigh, Zoe expressed her reluctant gratitude as she unpacked her laptop and powered it up. Two clicks and she'd pulled up her e-mail.

"Awesome," she exclaimed, all visions of stupid costumes fleeing from her mind.

"What? Your costume is there?" Meghan exclaimed.

Zoe grinned, pleasure surging through her as she plopped cross-legged on the bed and pulled her computer close.

"No. Even better. Dex is here."

"What's a Dex?"

"My lifeline to sanity," Zoe said, leaning back onto the cushy pile of pillows as memories washed over her. "We used to hang out. He was as much of a geek as I was, totally obsessed with Dungeons and Dragons, role-playing, that kind of thing. His parents own this hotel."

She scanned his note again and told Meghan, "I guess he's here this week to help out. That's how he got my e-mail addy, from the registration."

"So what're you going to do? Get some sexy times in? Don't you have enough on your plate already without dishing up distractions, too?"

An image of the hottie in the lobby flashed through Zoe's mind. That guy was all about sexy times. But Dex? She snickered. He'd been three inches shorter than her, shy to the point of stuttering and given his obsession with playing dress-up with other men, quite possibly gay. Do Dex? Hardly.

"Nah, Dex and I are just friends," she told Meghan, avoiding the sexual distraction rebuke. After all, she was quite capable of juggling two things at once. Especially if one of them had shoulders like the guy in the lobby.

"Dex rocks," she told Meghan. "I was bummed when we

lost touch after I left school. It'll be great to catch up with him, see what he's been up to."

She scanned the e-mail again, noting that he said he was visiting. That meant he'd left town, too. They'd have a lot of show-and-tell to share.

"Just don't lose sight of why you're there," Meghan chided. Then she started reiterating suggestions on how to find Gandalf. Zoe listened with half an ear as she did a Web search, trying to find out what Dex had been up to the past ten years.

A knock sounded. She set the laptop aside and told Meghan to hold on as she went to answer the door. The bellboy handed her a large box with a wicked grin. Zoe glanced at the label, Dressed to Thrill and rolled her eyes.

"Costume party," she told the snickering deliveryman.

"Uh-huh," he said as he pocketed his tip and sauntered away.

Zoe wrinkled her nose at his retreating back, wanting to point out that if she was in the market for thrills, they'd hardly show up in a brown cardboard box. Before she could, though, she heard Meghan's shout over the phone.

"Is it there? Is that the costume?"

Looking at the label again, Zoe shut the door and lugged the box over to the bed. "You've got to be kidding. You went through a place called Dressed to Thrill? Do I really want to open this, Meghan?"

"As tempting as it was to get you something wicked and fun like a spy costume, I went with Betty Boop," Meghan said with a laugh. "I figured that was your favorite cartoon. Betty's sexy and fun, and she's always involved in lots of different things. And she might shoot down those virgin rumors you are so obsessed with."

Zoe rolled her eyes again and ignored the insult as she

pulled her metal nail file out of her purse and started cutting through the packing tape. She pulled a large white garment bag out of the packing container and tossed what looked like a note and invoice back in the box, which she then shoved on the floor so she could lay out the bag.

"So how do I turn Betty Boop into a riddle that says career consultant-slash-business   manager-slash-troubleshooter-with-commitment issues?" she asked as she unzipped the bag.

Meghan snorted. "I didn't know about the career requirement when I ordered it. But in your case, you can just wear sneakers and carry your BlackBerry and a cap gun."

Zoe's grin faded to a frown when her fingers encountered leather. Betty didn't wear leather, did she? She pulled the hanger from the bag, holding the outfit out at arm's length.

"Holy shit." She dropped the hanger and jumped back a foot, staring in openmouthed horror at the slinky mound of black leather on her bed. Her eyes shifted to the rest of the outfit which had fallen from the bag when she pulled out the costume. A studded collar, black mask and riding crop.

Shock, fascination and an insane urge to giggle fluttered in Zoe's stomach as she stared.

"You should have gone with the spy costume. There's no way in hell I'm going down there in this." Zoe eyed the black leather again and couldn't hold back her laugh. "Although I have to admit, nobody would ever call me as a virgin again after I walked in dressed like a dominatrix."

3

"I CAN'T BELIEVE I'M doing this," Zoe groaned as she tugged the leather and lace skirt down over her fishnet stockings, trying to cover her butt. She stopped for the third time on her march down the hotel hallway, reluctant to take that final step into the elevator and commit herself to this joke of an evening. "I should have come down in my pajamas and called myself a dream analyst."

But, no. She'd shimmied and shoved herself into the leather getup. Why? Because her brother was counting on her. And, as Meghan pointed out, if she didn't, not only would she miss an important chance to track down Gandalf, she'd be seen as a cop-out. As a loser.

The elevator doors swooshed open. This was her last chance to back out. Zoe sucked in a breath, puffed out her cheeks and then shrugged. One last reminder that she didn't care what people thought of her, she exhaled sharply and walked in, turned around and hit the lobby button.

Alone in the elevator, she inspected her reflection. She'd refused to wear the thigh-high pleather boots. Instead, she'd substituted her own ankle boots. Sexy shoes were mandatory, even when offset by fishnets and studs.

The majority of the outfit consisted of the boots and a wide, ruffled leather-and-lace miniskirt, with its nod to modesty. The rest was a black leather bikini top, slender strips anchoring it to a studded choker on top, and crisscrossing to the tiny panties hidden by her skirt on the bottom. Studded cuffs and a leather crop completed the outfit.

At least, she assured herself as she tugged at the skirt again, her body was pretty well covered. If you counted fishnet and leather straps as coverage.

Way to make an impression after ten years. Realizing she was freaking out over the same people who'd judged her so rudely before, Zoe repeated to herself that she didn't give two good damns what they all thought. She pulled back her shoulders and stuck out her chest. Then she glanced down. Maybe not quite that much, she winced as she noted the spikes on the black leather and adjusted her spine. No point in damaging someone accidentally before she found Gandalf. And, she reasoned, she'd dressed Goth her entire three years at Central High. How was this so different? Still black, still filled with attitude. Just a little less…fabric. And this time she had a handy-dandy riding crop to deal with anyone who got snotty.

Snickering at that idea, Zoe patted the BlackBerry clipped to her waist. Since almost every troubleshooting job she'd taken in the past year had been in the communications field, it was the sole clue to her actual career.

To say nothing of her means of escape. Dex had said he'd contact her at some point tonight to get together. She just hoped it was during the party.

Fifteen minutes later and Zoe could only laugh and shake her head. What was the shelf life on immaturity? Twenty-eight years old and these people still acted like teenagers. You'd think the guys would have at least learned a few new pickup lines.

Tapping her crop against her thigh, she made her way through the loud, humid room.

"Do you charge by the hour?" one guy said as she turned sideways to try to get past him to reach the committee's table.

"You couldn't afford me," Zoe said with a wink and a wave of her crop. She recognized him as a football player. If he'd recognized her, he'd have been crossing his legs.

By the time she reached the table to sign in, she'd been hit on five times, insulted eight and even though nobody had recognized her, she'd been treated with the same disdain as she'd hated in school.

It really was just like old times.

She automatically tucked the hurt away, firmly enmeshed in her old screw-you attitude, and lifted her chin.

"Zoe Gaston, checking in," she said to the puppy dog across the table. The woman was sporting a full body of fur, floppy ears and black-nosed whiskers.

"Gaston?" The puppy ran her paw down the chart, found Zoe's name and, while her eyes were huge as she took in the black leather ensemble, she just smiled and handed Zoe her name tag. "Please step over to the photo booth."

"Why?"

"Everyone whose costume qualifies for the reunion contest has to have their picture taken."

"What're the qualifications?"

"That your costume doesn't give away what you really do for a living," the puppy said, and then she winked. "I'm guessing you don't support yourself with spankings?"

Zoe blinked in surprise at the smile and friendly joke, then she laughed and said, "Nah, spankings barely keep me in grocery money," before returning the grin and moving to the picture line.

Zoe said cheese. The photographer, who she recognized as her old P.E. teacher, gave her the clear signal and as she slid off the stool, he commented, "You're the best costume since Brad's."

"Brad Young?" she asked. "What's he dressed as?"

"A wizard. Great cape." With that, the guy turned to the next person, camera at the ready and Zoe forgotten.

Brad. Figured. All the signs had been pointing to Brad Young, and now he was dressed as a wizard. Didn't that say it all? Zoe shook her head. Of all possibilities, it had to be the guy who'd rejected her. She forced herself to quit the mental whine-fest. She'd been way out of her league with Brad ten years ago. She wasn't now. This time, she'd call the shots and he'd be grateful. She'd find him, maybe flirt a little. If he was Gandalf, she'd contact Zach, find out what he wanted her to do, then get the hell out of Dodge. And leave Brad Young panting in her dust. Perfect.

Her eyes peeled for a pointy hat, Zoe reviewed her plan for the night. Connect with Brad was number one for the Gandalf quest. She tapped her crop against her thigh as nervous anticipation shimmied in her belly. She couldn't wait to see the look on her old crush's face when he caught a load of what he'd given up to chase a pair of pom-poms.

Cautioning herself against getting too cocky or tunnel-focused that Brad was her man, she scanned the room. There were three other guys whose careers she hadn't managed to verify before the reunion. Since all she had to go on were their graduation pictures, she figured she'd watch for name badges and costume giveaways. Any guy sporting a joystick was on her follow-up list.

"Well, well. You still haven't found any color other than black, hmm?"

Chin high, Zoe turned around. Her jaw clenched as she forced her lips into a smile.

Candice Love. Central High's homecoming queen, head cheerleader and girl voted most likely to have the world bowing at her feet.

Lovely.

Zoe straightened her shoulders, cocked her hip to one side and lifted her chin. Attitude to the rescue.

"I could barely believe my ears when Julie told me you were here. Zoe Gaston, the geeky virgin." Candice gave a tinkle of icy laughter as she eyed Zoe up and down with artfully rounded blue eyes. "You did know this costume party was to guess your career, right? Not to try to deny your graduating title?"

Zoe inspected the blonde's costume, then raised a brow. "Really? And you realized it's 2009, right? Not 1999? Or has life been so bad since school that you're living in the past?"

Fair question, given that Candice was wearing a cheerleader costume. Not quite the same as the one she'd worn in school, instead of a *C* on her low-cut sweater, there was a picture of a bee wearing a crown and a bunch of tiny bees lined up like her court. What the hell? Queen-bee bitch was now a job designation? Contrary to Zoe's petty hopes, Candice hadn't sagged, uglified or turned into a toad in the past decade. Nope. Blondie was still trim, perky and pretty. Figured.

"I'm in costume," Candice dismissed. "Apparently we both held on to quite a bit of our high-school personas, hmm?"

Charming as always. Zoe decided then and there she wasn't giving Candice a second more of her time than she had to.

Stealing Gandalf out from under her nose would be her reward for resisting the urge to fling insults.

"Apparently," was all Zoe said, flourishing her riding crop with a quirk of her brow. "If you'll excuse me, I'm supposed to meet someone."

Blue eyes narrowed at the dismissal. Zoe took pleasure in brushing off the woman who so easily stirred up every insecurity she'd ever had.

Crop tapping against her thigh, Zoe made her way across the loud, overheated room and out the side doors into the dark garden, letting the pitch-black evening envelope her in obscurity. She breathed a deep, cleansing breath and closed her eyes. Two more breaths and she could feel her shoulders again underneath the ropes of tension.

Well. That'd been fun. Not.

Absorbing the serenity of the moonlit garden, Zoe took another deep breath and tried to pep-talk herself into going back into the ballroom. Gandalf was in there. She'd be damned if she'd let Candice and her pom-poms intimidate her into losing her edge.

"Whip me, beat me, make me attend a class reunion?"

Zoe spun around to face the owner of the low, male voice. She peered through the dark, only able to make out his costumed body, since his face was shadowed. Still, heat flared and a wide, appreciative grin curved her lips.

Helloooo, gorgeous.

Breathless, she stared. Leaning against the wall, the guy was pure sex appeal. She narrowed her eyes, trying to make out his costume. Tight leather pants, a loose shirt and a big-ass sword. Between the dim garden light and what looked like a wide mask à la Zorro, she could barely make out his face.

But his body was a work of art. Tall, lean, but well-muscled, all Zoe could think about was pressing herself against his chest and trying him on for size. A black cape completed the mysterious look.

"Having fun?" he asked, his question reminding her of his ordinal comment.

"Hardly. To tell you the truth, it would have taken a whip to get to me attend if I'd known it would be this bad," she admitted.

"Time heals all wounds?" he asked in a teasing voice.

"Or sharpens all claws."

"Interesting image coming from a woman wearing leather and studs," he teased, his tone low and husky, almost as though he had a cold or was disguising it along with his face. He had a faint accent, giving his sexually charged words an extra dose of romance. She couldn't tell from where, though.

But there was something familiar about him. Not surprising, given the circumstances, but still she wished she knew who he was. She eyed his cape and recalled the photographer's comment. But, even though it'd been ten years, this guy just didn't remind her of Brad.

"Who are you?" she asked.

"Aragorn."

She narrowed her eyes. Wasn't that a *Lord of the Rings* character? She scanned the costume again and tried to remember the movie. Unlike some of her friends, she hadn't read the books. Instead, she'd gone to see the hot, sexy hunk hero and that cute blond elf guy. She regretted not paying more attention to the names, but with all that eye candy, she'd been distracted.

"How about your real name?" she invited.

"Nah. It's a costume party. Go with the mystery."

Zoe debated. He *could* be Brad under that mask. Better yet, he could be Gandalf. Or was she just justifying her need to spend some time with a guy who got her thinking naked thoughts with just a few words?

"How about a break?" he suggested. "Catch your breath before you head back in to whip butts and make them beg."

He gave a charming, one-sided grin in response to her snort of laughter, then gestured to the path leading toward the rose arbor. "Maybe a walk in the moonlight?"

When he gestured, his cape fell back. She could clearly see the outline of his chest and shoulders beneath the soft flowing fabric of his shirt. Her breath caught. The sculpted muscles beneath the white cotton owed nothing to the costume and everything to Mother Nature. Broad shoulders, solid pecs and biceps that made her mouth water.

Sexy. Zoe swallowed hard, her body already aware, went on hyperalert. Her breasts swelled, nipples pressed arousingly against their leather restraints.

"A walk sounds tempting," she breathed, tucking her hand in his elbow. God, what could be more romantic? A moonlit walk in the gardens beside a gorgeous guy with a really big sword who got her hot with just the sound of his voice.

She slid him a sideways glance, but even close-up she couldn't make out his features. Between the dark night and the wide black mask wrapped around his upper face and tied behind his head like a bandana, all she could tell was that his hair was slicked back. Short? A wig? The way the mask was tied made it hard to tell.

Who was he? If he was Brad, he'd have said something, wouldn't he? But Brad was the only guy at Central High ever to really notice her. She tried to remember if he'd been this lean. Granted, it'd been ten years, but she'd remembered him as having more of a ballplayer build than a runner's physique.

They stepped off the patio and into the open garden. The cold evening air hit her almost-naked body. Zoe grimaced and instinctively stepped closer to the man's warmth.

So much for romance. She'd forgotten she was dressed up as the menacing man-eater.

"Here," he said shifting his cape.

She caught her breath, wondering if he meant to pull her under it with him. But he didn't. Instead he released the collar and swung it off, then wrapped it carefully around her shoulders.

"Thanks," she said quietly.

"You looked uncomfortable."

"I forgot how chilly it could get," she said.

"I meant in there," he said, gesturing toward the curtained windows of the ballroom. The noise was blunted out here, but they could still hear the occasional loud laugh, screech or drum roll.

"I forgot what it was like. Feeling like such an outsider," she murmured. "I didn't quite expect…"

"Were they rude?" His words were simple enough, but the anger underlying them made Zoe shake off her pity party and stare up at him. Now that he'd pulled off the cloak she could see the wide strength of his shoulders. But it was the set of his jaw that caught her attention. Stiff with anger, for all his calm words he looked like he might go back in there and…what? Give them a one-two-kapow?

Zoe snickered at her imagination. Then she realized she'd given too much energy to the responses in the ballroom. She hadn't cared what those people thought ten years ago, why should she now?

"It was no big deal," she said with a shrug. "More hits than barbs if you know what I mean."

"The guys hit on you?" he asked with a deep, husky laugh. "Figures. I mean, you're gorgeous. And your costume challenges every man in the room and makes all the women disappear into the wallpaper."

Zoe's breath caught in her chest. This guy oozed sex appeal the way Candice oozed bitchiness. It was a physical thing, intense and overpowering. It was a sexual energy that tempted. The kind that made her think of dark nights, warm breezes and naked bodies. And he thought she was gorgeous.

He'd given her his cape, growled in irritation over perceived slights and made her laugh.

Call her vain, but he'd had her at *gorgeous.*

As she stared up at him, wishing she could see the color of his eyes in the evening light, his laughter faded. His gaze narrowed and he stepped closer.

"You don't look like you believe me," he murmured, his words low and musical.

"I've been called challenging plenty of times," she admitted, her head spinning as her body reacted to the closeness of his. "But never gorgeous."

"But you are." He reached out, his hand fisted, and rubbed his knuckles over her cheek. Zoe damn near purred.

"Maybe you just have a leather fetish," she suggested.

"Maybe I'd like to try a few fetishes with you and see how they feel," he said, his words low and intense.

The image of the two of them naked except for his mask and her boots filled her mind. Zoe swallowed, her pulse racing so fast she felt as though it was going to pound its way out of her throat. Was he Brad after all? Confusion swirled through the desire filling her brain. Hadn't one of the twins mentioned Brad had gone to England? Was that an English accent? He obviously knew her. She couldn't imagine any other guy at the reunion would flirt with her like this.

His hand left her cheek. Zoe bit her bottom lip to keep from pouting. Then he wrapped both hands around the edges of the cape he'd draped around her shoulders.

The cloth still bunched over his fists, he used them to tilt her chin up.

"I'd want you even without the leather," he said.

Her grin was fast and wicked. "Naked, you mean?"

He groaned, then laughed. Zoe's heart tripped a little. So few guys could handle her smart mouth, let alone appreciate it while they were trying to make a move. But Mr. Supersexy? He just shook his head and grinned. His lips still curved with humor, he held her gaze captive as he lowered his mouth.

Her breath caught. Then her mind went blank.

His lips rubbed gently over hers. Warm, soft, intoxicating. Almost sweet, except for the sexual flare of heat zinging through her body. Her nipples hardened, her legs went lax. She grabbed his waist for support, her head falling back as he shifted from soft and sweet to hard and wild.

Zoe gasped, instantly aching and wet as his tongue took hers. She'd never had a kiss like this—so hungry and intense, she could barely keep up. Instead of trying, she gave herself over to the power of his demanding mouth. Let herself freefall with the swirling passion tightening in her belly.

Who knew the wrong costume could garner such a perfect prize?

DEX PULLED BACK from the kiss, his mind blown to bits. Damn. He'd finally found something—someone—to shut his always churning brain off.

"Come up to my room," he blurted out. Then he cringed. *Great, Drake. First time you've seen her in ten years and five minutes after saying hello you hit on her. You haven't even told her who you are and you're trying to get your best friend naked so you can nibble your way up and down her body.*

Her green eyes were filled with a heady combination of shock and desire. Her breath came in short bursts from her glossy, inviting lips.

Dex couldn't rip his eyes off Zoe. She was hot. Sexy, secure and so damned sassy. The eyes of an angel, a mouth to suit the leather lovingly encasing her body. And her taste. Pure ambrosia. He could get drunk on her taste alone.

So much for his comfortable lie of just wanting to reconnect with a friend. He wanted to connect with her, all right, but it had nothing to do with old times.

His hands, still under the cape, slid up her waist to the outside of her leather-encased breasts. He wanted to touch her. To see her. To bring all his fantasies to life. Dex had based his fantasy woman on Zoe. SweetCheeks, the kick-ass superheroine of his hit video game. Powerful, with her take-no-crap attitude and sexy body she fought the bad guys and saved his world.

But SweetCheeks had nothing on the woman in his arms, the woman he wanted to spend long, intense hours worshipping.

He couldn't believe his gamble had paid off. After her friendly-in-a-big-sister-kind-of-way e-mail response, he'd realized that he didn't want to waste this reunion with Zoe being friends. So he'd taken a chance with the costume.

figuring he'd feel her out first, then when she was hooked, he'd show her who he was.

Of course, that was before he'd felt her up instead. Now he felt like a jerk.

"I can't."

Huh? Had she read his thoughts? Dex frowned, his brow furrowed. "Can't?"

Oh, yeah. His room.

Yes, she could. Her body said she could. It was still pressed tightly against his, her legs cradling his thigh between them. Sure, there was a mile of fluffy skirt there, too. But he had a great imagination. He was picturing that gone.

Her hands still clutched his shoulders, fingers rubbing soft circles over the fabric of his shirt.

But her mouth said no. Dex sucked in a deep, painful breath and released his hold on her. Before he could step away, she angled her head. He recognized it as her challenge tilt.

"What?"

"I said *can't*. Yet. Not that I don't want to."

Dex's ego, and his dick, swelled.

"I have something I have to do before I can take off. But if you want to help me, I can get away faster. Then we can go somewhere. Get to know each other, hang out. You know, lose the mask and chitchat."

In other words, no free pass to sex, but they could spend some time together and see what came up. A grin splitting his face, Dex gave an eager nod. His hands immediately returned to her waist. He'd get her in a private room, show her who he was, then convince her to let him worship her body with his tongue.

"Anything," he agreed. "You name it."

"I have to find this guy," she said quietly.

"Sugar, I'm all guy," he teased. "Want proof?"

Her smile turned wicked. Pleasure shone in her bottle-green eyes as she stepped a little closer. She didn't rub against his straining erection. She didn't grab or fondle him. She just stood close enough so the heat of her body sent his reeling with desire. Obviously the queen of timing, she waited one heart-beat, then two. Then she raised a brow and, taking a deep breath so the leather tips of her bra brushed his chest, she smiled.

"Oh, I can tell that you're all man. I'd love to explore that fact in slow, careful detail."

Heat filled his body, slow, languid and intoxicating. Dex gave in to temptation and, hands on her leather-covered hips, he pulled her closer. Not as close as he wanted, but enough that he could feel the heat of her body against his.

"Who's the guy?" he asked, curious.

"I don't know his real name," she said softly, her fingers trailing up his chest, then back down to his belly. As if she wasn't paying much attention to what she was saying, she watched her fingernail swirl out a design on his belly. Dex stiffened his abs and gave thanks for his gym membership.

"You want some guy whose name you don't know?" he asked, starting to get a little jealous. Even wrapped in his arms, she still wasn't completely focused on him.

She laughed, a sound filled with wicked joy.

"No, no," she said as she hooked her index finger behind his belt buckle. Dex's eyes almost crossed. His dick went rock-hard in a heartbeat. "I know his name, I just don't know…what he looks like."

"Wander the halls yelling his name tomorrow," he suggested, barely hearing their words. All his energy, his entire focus, was on her finger and its proximity to his aching hard-on.

"I can't," she murmured, arching her back as he swirled designs on her warm flesh with his fingertips. "He's the reason I'm here."

Pulling his brain out of his pants, Dex tried to follow what she was saying.

"Sounds interesting," he said, then couldn't resist teasing, "Apparently you have a thing for mystery guys?"

She tilted her head to the side, giving him a long, amused look.

"I'm pretty sure I know who you are," she said with a husky laugh as she linked her fingers behind his neck.

"And you're cool with this?" he asked, unable to believe his luck. Yes! Years of lying to himself, of denying he had the hots for Zoe, dropped away. She was here, in his arms. And she wanted him as much as he wanted her.

"I wish we'd done this when we had a chance," she said softly.

"Oh, yeah. Me, too," he told her as, finally giving in to temptation, he leaned down to press a soft kiss on the sharp curve of her jaw. Dex breathed in her intoxicating scent, a citrusy vanilla that made his head swim. "I can't believe we didn't do this over and over again."

"Well, we tried."

Huh? Dex's mouth slowed as he tried to decipher her night-soft voice.

"I mean, the drive-in was a total disaster, but we could have given it another shot later. Maybe somewhere with less chance of your parents crashing."

Dex's mouth froze.

Drive-in? Parents?

His brain slowly kicked into gear.

Sonofabitch.

His vision blurred with anger, Dex released his hold on Zoe's hips.

Sure, he was wearing a mask. But it was still him. The man who appreciated her over-the-edge braininess. The guy who got her wicked sense of humor. The one who'd always considered her the sexiest gal he'd ever known, even back when she wore baggy black overalls and combat boots.

A part of him—granted, the part in his pants—had hoped she'd at least recognize him on some level. Or be intrigued enough, hooked enough, to put some effort into finding out who he was.

But, no. Her lips still wet with his kisses, she'd leaped to the most asinine conclusion possible.

She thought he was that dick, Brad Young.

4

AMID TABLES FILLED WITH chattering reunion members, giggling old friends and friendly couples, Zoe sat by herself in the hotel restaurant the next morning. She ignored the sideways looks and behind-the-hand snickers, although the pointing fingers were a little annoying. Obviously her costume had been a big hit, although not enough of one for anybody to actually come over and talk to her. Figured. She sniffed back the irritation and told herself it didn't matter. She shoved aside her pick-me-up pancakes and tapped her spoon on her teacup.

Snide classmates were nothing. What really mattered was what the hell had happened last night. One minute, she'd been hot and heavy with her very own masked marvel. The next he'd given her the heave-ho. An offhand excuse, a kiss on the cheek and whoosh, he'd flown off into the night.

Was it proximity to Central High that made guys ditch her mid-makeout session? The chilly Idaho air? If she'd had any doubts that she'd been locking lips with Brad, that move had squashed them. Apparently ten years and the guy still kissed and ran. The question was, was that his MO with all women? Or just with her?

"Ahem."

Zoe glanced at the table next to her. The elderly gentleman

there gave her a reprimanding look, then stared pointedly at her spoon. Oops. Tapping too loud.

Not wanting to further piss off the one nonsnickering face in the room, she set her spoon down and, after a sip, shoved her cold tea away.

She hadn't even managed to track down Gandalf after the masked hunk had left, either. By the time she'd returned to the reunion, the party had been moved to a local bar. She'd questioned the few people left, but all she'd managed to confirm was that, yes, Brad in his wizard costume had cut out early.

Where did that leave her?

Flummoxed and frustrated.

Which sounded like an up-and-coming garage band.

As if cued on protest, her phone sounded the gentle chimes of "Ode to Joy." Grateful for the distraction, Zoe grabbed it and pushed the necessary buttons to open the text messages. Then she winced when she read the one from Meghan.

Hey, Zoe. Any luck with the great wizard hunt? Zach's meeting with some bigwigs at Microsoft this week. You know how he feels about corporate America. This breaks my heart. He said he's just checking options, but I can tell he's upset. I asked him what he'd offer Gandalf if he ever found him and he mentioned a few things. I'm e-mailing you the list in case they might help your argument when you find the guy.

Shit. Poor Zach. That now-familiar twinge of guilt poked at Zoe. She squared her shoulders. She wasn't leaving this reunion without finding the solid information on Gandalf. Besides, after her hot-and-heavy in the garden with the masked hunk, she couldn't leave until she'd finished what he'd started.

Zoe took a sip of her iced water. Whew, she was a little warm at the memory of his mouth on hers, his hard, sculpted chest pressing against her breasts and the feel of his hard…muscles under her hand.

Focus, Zoe.

Next was a request that she reconsider the full-time job offer from her last consulting gig. *No, thank you.* It'd be career poison to tie herself to one single job, day in and day out. Or more correctly, tie some job to her. They'd regret it, and she'd be back to square one when they fired her. Maybe there was a twelve-step program for noncommitters anonymous?

With a sigh, she let the screen go black. She wasn't going to worry about work right now. Zoe scanned the room, clenching her jaw at the smug faces looking her way. She hated that they bothered her. Blinking quickly to banish the frustrated tears, she looked out the window. All she really wanted to do was find the masked hunk and get friendly again. Her shoulders slumped and she sucked in a deep breath to try to reel in the irritating emotional overload. Although, if she was honest, she'd admit it was probably pointless. After all, he'd already rejected her when he'd taken off last night.

God, she was even irritating herself with this self-pity crap. Twenty-four hours back in town and her confidence was toilet-height. Just like her glorious teens.

"Excuse me, Mr. Drake?"

Zoe's head whipped around, looking for Dex's dad. Or better yet, Dex himself. Hey, any friendly face would do.

Her eyes rounded as she stared at the hot guy from the lobby. He was focused on signing something for the restaurant manager. His hair was just as untamed coffee-hued wild waves as it'd been yesterday. His butt just as nice close-up as it had been bent over that cart. And his shoulders. Oh, yeah, she still wanted to run her fingers over the naked breadth of them.

Zoe pressed her hand flat against her tummy, glad now that she hadn't eaten anything. The food would have just gotten in the way of the horny butterflies dancing around in there.

Had the manager called him Mr. Drake?

Hottie with the nice ass from the lobby was Dex? Her old friend Dex? No way.

"Dex?"

At the sound of her voice, gorgeous guy turned to face her. Holy crap. That couldn't be her old friend. Could it? Tall, toned and hot? This guy looked nothing like her geeky buddy. But the eyes, she saw for the first time, were the same. A deep intense aquamarine.

"Dex," she repeated under her breath, her own eyes widening in shocked appreciation. He was definitely Dexter Drake, but my oh my, had he matured nicely.

He looked disconcerted. Tension flashed in his eyes, then with a visible shrug, Dex gave her a stiff smile. He said something to the manager before coming toward her.

Zoe's shoulders drooped. What? Was her old friend as uninterested in seeing her as the rest of her graduating class? Nah. No way. This was Dex. They'd always stuck together. Besides, he'd sent her the e-mail, said he wanted to get together. Shoving her paranoia aside, Zoe slid back her chair, smoothed her black leather skirt and rose to greet him.

Her gaze wandered over his body again, taking in the fit of his jeans over slim hips. His lightweight navy sweater was loose, hiding his chest, but his shoulders were broad and inviting. Her eyes traced the strong lines of his jaw where his hair waved back off his face. Zoe's heart thumped a little harder in her chest, reminding her to pull back her shoulders and be thankful for pushup bras.

Oh, yeah, she was definitely excited to see Dex.

"Hey," she said when he was a foot away. "I couldn't believe it when I got your e-mail. It's so cool that you're here."

The last words were said against his shoulder as, unable to help herself, she pulled him into a hug. It was like wrapping her arms around a very large, very well-muscled wall. Her breath caught in her chest, excitement swirling in her stomach.

He didn't even pat her shoulder, though. Zoe dropped her hands quickly and stepped back, trying not to look like plastering herself against his body had been a major turn-on.

She ignored the couple of catcalls and taunts from surrounding diners. Dex glanced around when one guy suggested she haul out the riding crop, but his expression didn't change.

"Hey, Zoe," he said, his words light, friendly.

"It's so good to see you again," she said, smile still hopefully bright. She inspected the face she'd thought she'd known as well as her own, amazed at how different he looked. Oh, the old Dex was there. Those intense, beautiful eyes with his lush, enviable eyelashes. The sharp angles of his face, just like his father's. The full lips she used to tease him about. Now, instead of wanting to offer him her black lipstick, they made her wonder how they'd feel against hers.

The air between them suddenly sparked with awareness. Zoe met his shuttered eyes. Lurking in his ocean-deep gaze was a heat she recognized. The same heat curled deep in her belly. She wet her lips, trying to calm her breathing.

"I can't believe how much you've changed," she blurted

out, trying to cover her lusty thoughts. "I mean, how many inches have you grown?"

Dex's mouth quirked, the shutter dropping from his eyes as they lit with wicked glee.

"Maybe we should finish saying hello before we discuss that," he said with a grin that made the horny butterflies in her tummy swoon.

"By all means," she said with a slow smile, leaning toward him as if the warmth of his body could relieve some of the sexual tension zinging through her system. His cologne, barely discernible over the cozy morning scents of breakfast and coffee, tugged at her memory.

Before she could place it, he stepped back. She blinked a couple of times, frowning as he put space between them as though she had a leftover case of cooties.

"You look great," he said. His tone was warm, though. Not cootie-wary. The look he gave her, like a gentle caress up the length of her body, was even warmer. It was as if he lit a fire in her body as heated awareness filled her. Maybe she'd imagined his hesitance?

"Thanks," she said. His gaze made her very aware of how low-cut her red sweater was and what an interesting view he must have from his height. Zoe didn't know whether to pull back her shoulders and smile. Or slap her hands over her half-naked chest and remind him that they used to climb trees together and plot to take over the world.

The naughty voice in the back of her mind suggested she combine the two, pull back her chest and ask him to climb on.

"Join me, please. Have a cup of coffee and tell me what's new in your life," she said. She couldn't tear her eyes from him as he sauntered over and took a seat. Wow. Who knew such a sexy hunk of manflesh had been lurking in such a, well, totally geeky nerd?

"What have you been up to?" he asked as soon as he sat. With a flick of his finger, he let the passing waiter know he wanted coffee. Zoe noted his absolute confidence, his easy command. His attitude said he clearly knew he was in charge and didn't expect his authority to be questioned.

Before she could answer, two guys from her class stopped at the table. They greeted Dex like a long-lost friend, invited him to a party and mentioned golf the next day. Her, they treated like a potted plant.

Zoe ignored them right back. She didn't care. She had an intriguing puzzle sitting across from her to focus on. She was too busy wondering what Dex had been doing and how he'd morphed into such a gorgeous man.

"Sorry about that," he muttered. "So you were telling me what you've been doing?"

Tearing her eyes from his very large, very strong-looking hands, Zoe forced herself to stop wondering how they'd feel taking charge of her body and focused on his question.

"Me? Not much. I'm a business consultant specializing in communication companies. Basically I troubleshoot. You know, check out the company, assess the problems, offer a pile of suggestions and take off."

"And how does that translate into whips and leather?" he asked with a grin, nodding his thanks to the waiter who poured his coffee.

"Whips and…" Oh, man. He'd seen her? Why hadn't he said anything? Zoe hadn't worried about sashaying around in her little leather bikini among her former classmates. After all, she didn't give a rip what they thought of her. But Dex?

She took a sip of cold tea to hide her nerves at the idea of him seeing her in such a revealing getup. Did he think it made her sexually aggressive? Did he like the idea? Was the riding crop a turn-on? Her breath lodged somewhere in her chest as she tried to figure out if she'd be excited or freaked if that was his reaction.

"I didn't realize you'd been at the party," she murmured, watching him doctor his coffee.

Dex's gaze flew back to hers. He fumbled the creamer a little, so it poured as much on the table as in his cup. "I wasn't."

Zoe frowned.

"I heard about the costume," he continued. "From some of the guys."

The guys. She glanced over at the men, now sitting at a crowded table, who'd stopped to talk. Unlike her, Dex's geek status hadn't kept him out of the popular circles. Zoe pulled a face. "I guess it's a toss-up who the bigger gossips are—the guys or the gals."

He just gave a half smile and shrugged. That he wouldn't meet her eyes made Zoe wonder if the gossip had been rude. Zoe pressed her lips together, the sting of rejection a little harder to ignore this time. It wouldn't be the first time her classmates had made obnoxious comments about her. Dex used to try to hide them from her back in school, too.

Her heart gave a little sigh at the sweet gesture.

Despite the hurt, the mention of gossip sparked an idea. Everyone talked to Dex. Which meant he might know something about Gandalf. Or at least who was doing what since school.

"So…" she said slowly, leaning back in her chair just a little. His gaze intensified into molten aqua, sliding over her chest with a heated caress that made her glad her sweater was a thick one. Zoe swallowed hard and shifted a little in her chair. Wetting her lips, she forced herself to speak normally. "I have to admit, it's a little bit of a shock to find you here in town. I though the only person who wanted out of this Podunk town more than I did was you."

"I don't live here," he told her, the warmth leaving his eyes as he gave her an offended look, as though she'd just accused him of selling out. Which, she supposed, she had, given his previous antipathy to the place. "I'm just in town for the week helping out while my parents vacation."

"That's cool that they can count on you to help out. Where are you living then?"

"I'm…" His hesitation confused her.

"It's not that complicated a question," she said dryly. "Not like I'd asked for all the down-and-dirty details of your love life or anything."

Although it was tempting.

Dex shot her a weird look. If she didn't know better, she'd call it cold. Was he pissed that she'd teased him? Nah. She was just reacting to the temperature in the room, filled with obnoxious classmates.

"I'm between places right now," he said, his words clipped.

"Like moving to a new apartment?"

"Like trying to figure out what state I want to live in. I was living in Boston doing some I.T. work, but haven't decided exactly where I want to relocate to."

She gave a silent *oh*. A lot of free time. No job tying him to a residence. Bouncing from state to state. No wonder he'd gotten all pissy over the question. Was Dex out of work?

Suddenly she felt every hour of the intervening ten years. Before, she'd have nagged and cajoled until he told her everything. Now she felt as if she was trespassing just by asking. Unsure if it was his don't-touch attitude or her imagination, Zoe changed the subject.

"Well, it sure is my luck that you ended up in town the one week I'd be here." She wanted to reach across the table and lay her hand over his. Ten years ago, she wouldn't have hesitated. Just like nagging him for details, she'd have dived right in.

For the first time, she regretted her inability to commit to anything, even something as simple as staying in touch with an old friend. She should have kept up with Dex. Even an e-mail here and there would have bridged this gap.

Of course, ten years ago she wouldn't have been in a serious case of lust sitting across from Dexter Drake. Irritated with how awkward she felt, Zoe forced herself to ignore her desire to run her fingers over his hand, slide them up his arm and cup his biceps to see if he was as hard as she thought. And any thoughts of sliding and cupping anything else to test for hardness were strictly off-limits.

"Lucky for both of us," he said with a lopsided grin. The smile was like a kick in the rear for Zoe. He'd had that same grin as a kid. A kid who'd been her best friend. A kid who was a year younger than she was and hardly interested in a flaky older woman with commitment issues.

Disgusted with herself, Zoe hunched her shoulders a little as she tapped her fingers on the table. Focus. She had a reason for being here. She needed to pay attention to that and quit fantasizing about doing the guy sitting across from her.

"Dex," called a guy as he left the restaurant. "Watch out for her riding crop."

Zoe glared. Dex ignored him.

"So you've obviously caught up with everyone, huh?" she said with a sniff.

"Not so much. I've talked to a few of the guys. Had a couple of propositions from those crazy redheads. That's about it."

His grin was wicked this time, inviting her to share his amusement that two gals who'd never have given him the time of day back in high school were trying to get in his pants now.

Zoe's answering smile was little more than a curl of her lip. Apparently lusting after Dex required a club card or something.

"But you've heard who's doing what? Like what jobs the guys have and stuff?"

Dex's smile dimmed. He leaned back in his chair, crossed his arms over his chest. "Why? You shopping for a specific guy-job combination?"

"You could say that," she said with a shrug. "Not for me though. I'd heard a rumor that a local celebrity is actually a part of our graduating class and wanted to talk to him."

Dex frowned. "So why don't you just find him and talk?"

"He uses a pseudonym."

It was as though he froze. Zoe's brows drew together as she watched. Dex's expression didn't change. He didn't move at all. And yet, he felt glacier-cold.

"Like, what? A writer or something?"

"Sort of." She glanced around, noting a few former class-mates seated at nearby tables. She scooted her elbows on the table and leaned closer so she could whisper. "He creates video games."

DEX STARED, HIS BRAIN racing. He took care to keep his expression blank, though. What the hell? How had she heard what his alter ego did? And more important, why did she want him?

Besides the fact that Dex's entire career shift hinged on keeping Gandalf's true identity secret, he wouldn't tell her even if he could. Last night she'd thought he was Brad and now she wanted his alter ego? What was up with that? Call him a selfish guy, but he wanted Zoe to want him for himself.

Sure, he knew he'd been taking a chance last night, showing up in disguise and making out with her. Even though he'd been really careful in his costume, pulled back and hidden his hair, stayed in the shadows and let a hint of the Boston accent he'd picked up from his coworkers creep into his voice, he'd still hoped…what? That she'd see through his hidden identity and jump into his arms, claiming unrequited lust? Stupid. But still, he didn't know what bothered him more, her oblivion to his actual identity or that she'd mistake him for that jerk, Brad.

He'd spent most of high school jealous of Zoe's crush on Brad Young. He'd finally had his first kiss with her, the hottest, sexiest tangling of tongues he'd ever experienced. And she'd called him by that jerk's name. So, yeah, he was jealous. He wanted Zoe to see him as a man. An equal. And dammit, this time she was going to. He'd just tell her that it'd been him last night and they could pick up at the half-naked point and go from there. Sure, she'd be irritated, but the heat in her eyes gave him hope that the irritation would fade fast in the face of lust.

But first, he needed to know why she was interested in Gandalf. So he gave a shrug and shook his head.

"No clue who that might be," he told her. "I thought you did consulting, though. Not headhunting. Who's this guy? Why are you looking for him?"

He watched the disappointment wash over her face. She glanced at her phone, then gave a little grimace. "It's not work, it's personal," she told him.

Personal? Dex leaned forward to ask her just how personal. Before he could say anything, though, one of her ex-classmates stopped at their table.

"Dex, just thought you'd want to know there's some craziness in the lobby," the guy said. Dex couldn't remember his name but didn't figure it mattered. From the lusty look in his eyes, he'd really come to flirt with Zoe.

"Craziness?"

"Bunch of reunioners are signing up for this afternoon's limbo contest. I guess someone thought it'd be fun to spice it up a little. Now it's being billed as naked limbo." The guy, thirty pounds overweight, his pre-balding head gleaming in the morning sunlight, grinned at Zoe. "Of course, if you're playing, I'll have to play, too."

Dex snorted, both at the guy still attempting his clumsy flirtation and the reunion idiocy. Naked limbo? Who the hell thought this shit up? And why did he have to deal with it? Then he remembered. He was the Drake in charge. Damn.

Promising to check into it, he finally got rid of the guy.

"What's wrong?" Dex asked, seeing the annoyance on Zoe's face.

"He was one of the guys talking shit last night. Now he thinks I'll forget? I hate games and lies," she said with a roll of her eyes. "These guys talk one thing behind your back, then flirt to your face like they think they'll get lucky. They were like that in school and they haven't changed."

Dex's shoulders clenched. He knew she was referring to the drive-in incident. When word had got out that she was going on a date with that jerk, Brad, everyone had fallen all over themselves to act like her friend. When the date tanked, they'd used both her sudden notoriety as an excuse to publicly skewer her as only teenagers could. He took in the angry hurt in her green eyes. Damn. He'd always hated seeing Zoe upset. Maybe this wasn't the time to reveal the truth about his little subterfuge last night. But he had to tell her the truth. Didn't he?

"That's one of the things I like best about you, Dexter," she said, leaning forward with her hands pressed to the table in a way that made her sweater gape intriguingly. "You've always been honest with me. Unlike some jerks, you don't play games."

Dex's mouth watered at both the view and the sexy sound of his name on her lips. After last night, he'd had a driving need to hear her say his name. In conversation. In acknowledgment. In bed.

Especially in bed.

His ego, still smarting that she hadn't recognized him, demanded no less.

His brain, remembering how fast her temper flared, cautioned him against saying anything that would have her thinking he'd played her last night.

And his dick? His dick didn't care. All it wanted was for him to hold her against his body again. To get her naked and see how many ways he could make her come before losing himself in the hot, wet pleasure of her body.

Then the rest of her words sank in. Honest? Always?

Shit.

His conscience and his body went to war. If he told her, he'd never feel her body against his again. She'd give him that same look, the resigned hurt mixed with disdainful anger. He much preferred the hot, sultry look of curiosity in her eyes now.

To hell with his conscience. He wanted to take her up on that look.

"Mr. Drake?"

Dex yanked his gaze from Zoe's to glance at the hotel manager. "Sir, we have a problem at the pool."

"The pool?" Dex glanced out the window. It had to be forty degrees outside.

"Mrs. Drake was hosting her weekly pinochle club. Somehow, it changed into a…" The man glanced at Zoe, then grimaced and lowered his voice. "A séance by the pool. Apparently someone panicked and fell in. It sparked a, well, rather enthusiastic reaction from the other attendees and now the pool is filled with octogenarians who are rapidly turning blue."

Dex closed his eyes and sighed. Why hadn't his parents warned him that it wasn't the inn that'd be so much trouble to watch over? It was his grandma.

Zoe's snicker was quiet, but Dex heard it anyway. He gave her a mock glare. She giggled. "I forgot how much fun your grandma was," she said. Something shifted in her eyes. The heat cooled, replaced by affection and something else. Memories, maybe?

"I guess I need to go fish some people out of the pool," he said, nodding to the manager, who left with a relieved sigh. Dex couldn't figure out why the change in her expression bothered him. "I'm sorry to cut our reunion short."

"I have to go anyway," she told him. Then she leaned forward and laid her hand over his. Warm tingles danced their way up his arm and straight down to his crotch. Then, before he could turn his hand over to take hers, she pulled away.

She stood slowly. Dex's gaze slid over her body as she rose. Damn, she was beautiful. He was developing a major fetish for leather. He wanted to wrap his hands over the sweet curve of her hips, pull her against him and nibble his way across her belly.

"It was good to see you, Dex." He met her gaze, saw the confusion, then a reluctant decision in the beautiful depths. "Reunions are supposed to be for catching up with old friends but we both know you're the only one I had here. I'm glad to have a chance to renew that friendship."

Dex frowned. Her message was clear. She planned to let the chemistry between them go unexplored.

So he let her go. He knew Zoe. Her words said *not interested,* but those were just words. He looked into her eyes, saw the heat and interest lurking beneath the amusement. Yeah. They'd talk again soon. As soon as he figured out the next move in the game.

"See ya," she said, grabbing her phone then sauntering away as though she didn't have a care in the world. He watched her stop at the hostess's desk and talk to the woman there, gesturing to the table and giving him a wicked smile. He grinned back, amused at what was obviously girl talk when his hostess shot him a wide-eyed look of laughter. Then, as if she had no idea his gaze was cemented on her butt, Zoe left the restaurant in a slow, hip-swinging strut that made his mouth go dry. Dex lifted his cup of coffee to his lips, as if the caffeine might restart his brain.

Her words said *no.* Her hips said *maybe.*

Game on.

5

INEXPLICABLE SADNESS tangled with confused lust as Zoe sashayed across the lobby toward the elevators. She had to force herself not to turn right around and run back into the restaurant to beg Dex to forget they'd once been best friends and do her on the table.

But that'd be crazy. Because this was Dex. It was one thing to lust after a masked hottie who kissed her crazy in the dark. It was another to choose lust and risk her friendship—granted an old and not well-maintained friendship, which was beside the point—over it.

After all, she hadn't had many friends in her life. So it would be stupid to risk losing one, wouldn't it? Even if it had been ten years since she seen or heard from Dex and she wasn't sure if he still counted as a friend or not. Did it count if she didn't feel friendship so much as intense, powerful and gut-clenching desire?

And what kind of friend was she that she'd let the distraction of wondering if Dex's hands were as talented as they looked stop her from prodding, poking and getting the details of what he was actually up to these days? For a brief second, she wondered if Dex could be Gandalf. But then she shook her head. Nah. For one thing, he'd been working in I.T. last year. And second, Dex had always been the ultimate geek. A math and science whiz, but totally uncreative and shy. Definitely not the "develop a *fantasy* video game" kind of guy.

From the tiny bit he'd revealed, he was quite possibly unemployed. Broke? Those big dreams of success he'd been so determined to see to fruition as a kid, were they trampled in the ugly dust of reality? Maybe that was why he'd been so weird at first? Was he embarrassed? Zoe's heart sighed. Oh, man. Poor Dex. Her steps slowed. Maybe she could help him? Sure, she was used to working with big companies, but that didn't mean she couldn't adapt her skills to troubleshoot a single career, right? That's what she was doing for Zach, after all.

The image of Dex's sexy eyes, crooked grin and those incredible shoulders flashed through her mind. A lusty kind of nervousness took hold in her stomach, the kind of nerves that nagged a gal to go lingerie shopping before a first date. To endure the agony of waxing. To giggle idiotically, carefully plan serendipitous encounters and spend hours wondering how he kissed.

Which was crazy. This was her old friend. She wanted to help him because she cared. It wasn't like she was coming up with some ploy to get him naked and have her way with his body until they both collapsed in screaming ecstasy.

Not really.

That decided, Zoe grinned and spun around to return to the restaurant.

And ran face-first into a wide, bulky chest.

"Watch out," a deep male voice said as two beefy hands grabbed her shoulders to keep her from falling on her butt.

Winded, Zoe tilted her head back and blinked a couple of times. Then she frowned and blinked again.

"Brad Young?" she asked.

No way. It looked like her old crush. The captain of the football team and the first guy to feel her up. The blond hair was supershort, just as thick as ever and impeccably styled. The boyish face was still handsome. And the body? Zoe's gaze flicked over the fleshy arms and broad chest. The decade hadn't really done this body good.

"Yeah, I'm Brad," he said, letting go of her arms. "And you are…?"

Zoe took a step back, a little frown still creasing her brow. She gave him a second, longer look. Her hands lifted in the air, about a foot from his shoulders, measuring.

She wiggled her toes in her boots. The same boots she'd been wearing the night before. The four-inch heels brought her height to five-ten. But she still had to tilt her head way back to see Brad. Dropping her hands to her waist, she tapped her fingers on her hips.

Eyes narrowed, she once again dropped her gaze down his body. He wasn't fat, by any means. But he did have that I-just-work-out-my-arms-and-drink-lots-of-beer look. Unable to help herself, she eyed his zipper. Unlike Dex's jeans, which definitely had an intriguing bulk to them, Brad's khakis lay flat and smooth.

Like a Ken doll.

Brad wasn't the masked hunk. Her stomach sank into her toes as she worked through the panicked realization that she'd made out with a total stranger last night. And loved it.

"Babe? I'm glad you know who I am, and I'd love to know who you are. But you've got to say something." Laughter, not necessarily kind, rang in the low voice.

Pulling her thoughts off her makeout session and back to the conversation, Zoe's gaze flew back to Brad's. Gag. She'd forgotten that he called every girl *Babe*. Even in her crush-induced excitement over him, she'd realized ten years ago it was his way of not having to remember a girl's name.

His grin was wide and toothy, like a man trying out for a used-car-salesman job. Zoe forced her mouth to curve.

"Zoe Gaston," she finally said.

"No way!" His brown eyes rounded and he looked her over as though he was trying to figure out where she'd hidden the rest of her chubby, black-clad teenage self.

"Way," Zoe shot back, her smile growing stiff. "How have you been?"

"Awesome. I'm awesome, of course," he murmured, as though barely aware of his words. Instead his entire attention was focused on her. His eyes did a slow perusal of her body from the top of her tousled hair to the pointed tips of her boots. Zoe felt as if she was being visually groped.

She should be thrilled. One-hundred-percent attention from Brad Young had ranked right up there with perfect SAT scores and a date for the prom at the top of her high-school goals.

Instead, she felt like taking a shower.

She sighed, imagining her teenage heart deflate like a punctured balloon. She wanted to toss out an excuse and split. But her tapping fingers played a beat over the cell phone in her front pocket, reminding her of Meghan's message.

Brad was still the front-runner in the Who Is Gandalf quest. Which meant she needed him.

"I heard you were here and looking hot. Now I see it for myself. I'm sorry I missed you last night. I take it your whips-and-chains getup was in answer to that virginity problem?" he asked with one of those wink-wink-nudge-nudge leers.

"Guess you didn't need ol' Number Eighty-Nine to help you handle that."

He gave a jolly guffaw. Kind of like a perverted Santa Claus. Zoe knew her mouth was hanging open, but she couldn't help it. The guy still referred to himself by his football number?

"So how do whips and leather play into your job?" he asked, stepping closer. "I'll bet the details are juicy."

"Not really," she muttered as she took a small step backward. After all, she didn't need him enough to turn the visual gropes into the real thing.

Zoe wanted to turn and walk away from the oozing smarm. But Brad was her best bet in the quest for Gandalf. All her research so far, as well as the gossip she'd gathered, indicated he was the obvious candidate. So she pulled out her fallback defense. Attitude. She cocked her hip to one side, tilted her chin and gave Brad a wink worthy of Mae West. Pretending she was tapping her riding crop instead of her phone, she took charge of the discussion.

"I was sorry to miss you last night, too. I really wanted to see your costume. Someone said you were a wizard?" she asked with a smile. She threw in an attempt at fluttering her lashes for good measure. "Since I missed out, you'll have to fill me in. What are you doing these days?"

Brad frowned, peering at her as though he was trying to figure out what was wrong with her eyes. Zoe quit fluttering. "These days?" he asked blankly. "Same thing as always. I'm playing the game, ya know?"

Aha. She gave a relieved sigh. He *was* Gandalf.

"The game?" she asked ingeniously.

"You know—the game. Life is all about strategy. I put my

talents as Central High's football captain and class president to good use. First in college when I got my degree in computer science, then later, making a fat pile of money."

Zoe kept her smile in place, but cocked her head to one side and gave him a "huh?" look. How did that apply to video games? Gandalf hadn't created any sports games.

"So what, exactly, does that mean you're doing now?" she probed, her amiable smile slipping a little. She wanted to know if he was the video-game wizard or not. Because if he wasn't, she could get the hell away from him and his leer. God, what kind of idiot had she been to crush so hard on this blockhead?

"That's a secret, remember?" he said with a loud chuckle as he pulled her close for an over-cologned bear hug. Zoe grimaced against his chest. "You're just as sneaky as you are cute, huh? Trying to figure out what I do to win the reunion challenge."

"No, really—" Zoe started to protest.

Before she could do more than peel her face off his polo shirt and stutter, a cold laugh ricocheted around the room like a Stealth icicle.

"How sweet," Candice said as she glided over. Her entourage, including the redheaded twins and a dozen other perky-looking people, followed close behind. Candice gave Zoe a snide look, her eyes pure blue frost. Her entourage watched in rapt curiosity, waiting for Candice to beat Zoe over the head with a pom-pom or something.

Zoe sighed. No wonder she'd hated school.

"It's like going back in time," Candice murmured. "You chasing after the unachievable."

"And you, determined to win by any means possible," Zoe shot back.

The blonde gave a toothy grin, beauty queen to geek. "Of course, you have your own means, don't you? Leather, wasn't it?"

"I left my riding crop on the bedside table," Zoe deadpanned.

"Next to your leather bikini?" Brad asked, intrigued enough to risk stepping into the simmering catfight.

"Cute," Candice said at the same time.

Knowing from experience there was no point in trading ugly for ugly, Zoe offered them both a bland smile.

The blonde looked like a woman who'd just spent the morning in the salon: perfect hair, perfect skin, perfect body. She gave Zoe a smirk, then, stepping between her and Brad, placed her pink-taloned hand on the stud's chest and leaned close to kiss his cheek.

"I hope I didn't keep you waiting," she asked him.

Brad blinked a few times, a frown etching deep furrows in his forehead. "Huh?"

Zoe narrowed her eyes. Twenty-four hours and the cheer-leader had already bagged him? Or was she just trying to give Zoe that impression? No matter. Candice could have him. Or at least, have his body. It was his career Zoe wanted.

"I sent you an e-mail," Candice murmured, leaning closer to him and tilting her head to block Zoe from the conversation.

Brad's blue eyes blurred a little with confusion. Or maybe it was something else, given that Candice was squishing her boobs against his arm.

"I signed it SweetCheeks," she heard Candice whisper.

Brad's gaze cleared; a wicked grin split his face. "Gotta give props to a woman who knows her games," he said.

Heart speeding up, Zoe took an involuntary step forward.

"Brad," she started to say.

Before she could spit out anything else, though, Candice tucked her hand into his beefy arm and leaned her head against his shoulder. "Breakfast?"

"Sure," he said, his gaze glued on her cleavage.

"Zoe, I'll catch you later," he tossed off as Candice dragged him away. The entourage followed silently, although a few of them cast sympathetic looks Zoe's way.

Ignoring the pity, Zoe watched in futile silence as Candice stole Brad away from her. Again. As the couple reached the restaurant, the blonde turned and shot Zoe a gloating look, one brow raised in taunting triumph.

ZOE GLANCED THROUGH THE window into the dining room, noting the gathering of her ex-classmates and their coziness. She needed to talk to Brad. To talk to a few people, actually. But not in there. All she'd get if she tried to join the stupid round of games they were playing this afternoon was more snide snootiness from Candice or the pitying glances of the other classmates. No, thanks. She kicked a rock, watching it tumble across the leaf-strewn cobblestones with a frown.

"Now that's no way to treat such pretty boots."

She spun around, wincing as she found the owner of the voice. An elderly woman sat on garden stool, pruning the dead wood off an ugly bush. Her big floppy hat shaded her parchment skin from the late-afternoon autumn sun.

"Sorry, I didn't startle you, did I?"

The woman shook her head, her stare making it clear she did expect an explanation for the tantrum, though.

"I'm just frustrated," Zoe blurted out as she tucked her cell phone into her jacket pocket along with her hands. Damn, she'd forgotten how cold Idaho falls were. "Coming to this reunion was a mistake."

Obviously, so was taking this walk. Knowing she needed to move, she'd gone straight up to her room after her run-in with Candice and Brad, aka Barbie and Ken, and grabbed her jacket. Now she was making her way through the garden toward the bare hill just outside the hotel property.

"Why?" the lady asked, unfazed by Zoe's odd sharing. "Is it not what you hoped? Or too close to what you remembered?"

Zoe made a noncommittal sound, not sure how to say she'd had no hopes and the memories had sucked. Except of Dex. Those memories had been great.

She frowned, looking closer at the elderly woman. Recognition clicked into place. "Mrs. Drake?"

"Yes, indeed. And you're Zoe, aren't you?"

Eyes huge, Zoe looked down to see if she had a name tag on. "How'd you know?"

"Dexter always had a soft spot for you," the older woman said. Spry as someone half her age, she bounded from the stool and strode over to Zoe. "You're taking a walk? I'll join you."

Trying to decipher what a soft spot meant in teenage-boy speak, Zoe nodded and checked her steps to accommodate the octogenarian.

"I heard you had a séance earlier," Zoe said, changing the subject as she stepped through the well-tended white picket fence onto the path through the wild overgrowth around the outside of the inn's property. The cold autumn air had the biting scent of fallen leaves, decaying flowers and bitter cold. "I was with Dex when they told him about it. He seems to be handling running the inn really well." Then Zoe slid a sideways glance at the snickering older woman, both to gauge how much to say and also in wonder. Had she gone in the pool, too? "Dex has….changed."

"Well, that's not all bad, is it?" Mrs. Drake asked with a naughty laugh that seemed totally out of place in a grandmother. Yeah, Zoe was pretty sure she'd gone swimming. "I mean, that boy used to play dress-up, if you remember. I worried about him for a while."

Zoe blinked, wondering why. Dex had seemed like a dream kid to her. Good grades, helped out when he was asked. Sure, he'd bitched and moaned a bit, but he'd never caused his parents any real trouble.

"Did the two of you have a nice little visit?" the woman asked as she took Zoe's arm to step over a fallen branch on the path.

"Visit? It was…" Weird? She'd spent most of it lusting after her old friend. Not that she'd tell his grandma that. "It was a little awkward, I guess. We've fallen out of touch, you know?"

"True friendship requires a little work, of course."

Guilt tickled Zoe's spine at the truth of those words. She should have stayed in touch. Being back here, seeing Dex, reminded her of how much she'd appreciated him. But like everything in her life, she hadn't been able to hang on longterm. "We used to be best friends. We're obviously not now, but we should still be comfortable with each other, right? Except it was all, like I said, weird."

"Things change," Mrs. Drake said sagely. Then she shot Zoe a sharp look and said, "It's easy to use that as an excuse to let go. After all, they can be changed back, of course. If you want to do the work."

They'd reached the edge of the inn's property and the gate leading to a small stone cottage. The older woman gave Zoe a smile and said, "It was good to see you again, Zoe. Be sure to visit me while you're here. I like you."

Zoe blinked, then watched until Mrs. Drake was safely inside her cottage. Well, at least one person liked her. Somehow, that was as much a talisman as the attitude her riding crop gave her.

Zoe trudged through the heavy growth of still-green weeds and overgrown bushes up a hill. Huffing at the exertion, she frowned at the idea that maybe she'd brought some of this on herself, but she didn't slow down. She'd had to get out of the hotel, away from the excited squeals and annoying reunion festivities. Far, far away from the sight of Candice and Brad holding court with the popular people.

Fitting in had never been a goal of hers. But then, she'd always had Dex to make her feel safe. Accepted. And now? Now she was lonelier than ever. And it was her own fault. The truth was like a stinging slap. Quick, unexpected and shocking. Zoe pressed her lips together to keep tears from falling.

Was it laziness that had lost her Dex's friendship? Or fear?

Zoe grimaced, shoving her hands deeper into her coat pockets as she continued up the hill. How fun! She got to revisit her unhappy past and discover she was a hypocrite, all in the same week.

Doing what she always did when faced with dealing with her emotions, Zoe avoided it. Instead, she focused on the Gandalf puzzle. Brad was still the front-runner, but the masked hunk was also a possibility. He'd been dressed in a *Lord of the Rings* costume, after all. Maybe that was part of his riddle?

And she was positive now that the masked hunk was definitely not Brad. Sure, they were about the same height. And it'd been dark, and the sexy kisser had been disguised. But she was still sure. The masked hunk had been lean muscles. Brad was muscular, but more bulky. The voice was different, too. To say nothing of the attitude. The masked hunk had been interested, but still hesitant. Zoe had the feeling that if Brad had got his hands on her leather-clad body, nothing would have stopped him this time.

So who the hell had she made out with?

Zoe climbed over a fallen log, the rough wood catching the heel of her boot so she almost fell. Righting herself, she glanced up. There it was. Nestled between two large branches in an oak tree that was rapidly shedding its yellowing leaves. The tree house she and Dex had made when she was fifteen.

Bombarded by memories and emotions, Zoe plopped down on the fallen log and stared at the rotting wood of her teenage haven. Right there in the fork of those huge limbs, she and Dex had planned their future. They'd lamented the lame teachers and unchallenging curriculum. They'd brainstormed revenge on everyone who'd ever hurt her feelings. One time, she remembered with a little sniff, Dex had found her there in tears, hiding away from the world after her parents had died. He'd climbed up silently, held her, then wiped her face with the sleeve of his hoodie. She'd even shared her crush on Brad, then her heartbreak over his ugly behavior after their one date gone bad.

What a difference ten years made. Before, she'd been thrilled when one guy paid her any attention.

And now?

Three guys on her hands. One of them had given her the hottest kiss she'd ever had. One she needed for her brother's business success. The third was off-limits. Not only because he was her friend, but because Dex was the long-term type.

His being back here helping his parents, his connection with his grandma, those were proof that Dex wasn't a do-him-and-run kind of guy.

Of all the problems she'd imagined when she'd agreed to attend the reunion, this wasn't anywhere on the list. Zoe shook her head in disbelief. Who'd have thought it?

Zoe Gaston, the girl most likely to die a virgin. Chasing after three guys. And it didn't look like she was going to catch any of them.

She'd come back looking to use her past to do one selfless thing, secure a future for her brother. And what had she found? Failure, at its finest. Figured.

IRRITATION dogging him like a head cold, Dex stomped through the garden adjoining the hotel and his parents' house. He let himself into his childhood home, glaring at the hotel before he slammed the front door.

What a pain in the ass. First he'd spent the morning over-caffeinating while replaying his talk with Zoe. As much as he couldn't stop thinking about her, he also couldn't stop wondering what the hell she wanted with his alter ego. Sure, he wanted her wondering about him. But in an I-want-to-strip-this-guy-naked-and-do-him-eight-ways-from-Sunday kind of way. Not to track him down for a job.

But instead of finding her to continue their discussion, he'd had to deal with a half-dozen run-ins with old classmates, all of whom were thrilled to see him. Of course, the greetings were always followed by requests for deals on their rooms, free access for parties and other varied and sundry examples of why they thought he was useful.

Add to that having to chastise his own grandmother for

leading a skinny-dipping jaunt in the barely heated pool, the reunion committee's constant requests, a missing produce delivery, a plumbing problem and a lost toddler, all before noon, had nicely rounded out a sucky morning.

Coming back for this reunion had been a stupid idea. He didn't know the first thing about successfully running the hotel. He still couldn't stand most of the users he'd gone to school with. And he'd been an idiot to think he and Zoe could pick their friendship back up. A bigger idiot to dream they could actually hook up. He should have learned by now to save his wild imagination for his video games.

He passed through the kitchen, barely noticing the ancient avocado-hued appliances and gold-flecked formica counters. His parents spared no expense on the hotel, but he was pretty sure the house hadn't changed since he'd been born.

He grabbed a soda from the fridge and headed for his laptop. Zoe's question about Gandalf was nagging at him. Why was she looking for the gamer?

A movement caught his attention. Stepping over to the dining-room window, he watched a figure make its way down the hill behind the house.

Zoe.

Bundled all in black, from her knit cap to her peacoat and on down to the wicked-looking boots he'd dreamed about the night before, she looked lonely. The only spots of color were her scarlet scarf and her cold-washed cheeks.

Even from far away, she turned him on.

He'd wanted her for most of his teenage life. He'd dedicated many a fantasy to her. He'd finally tasted her and found out that, unlike most dreams, she was even better in real life.

So what was he going to do? Pout like a spoiled brat

because winning her wasn't easy? Or take a shot at an opportunity of a lifetime?

His straining erection urged the shot. His damaged ego urged restraint. Ever the mediator, he searched his mind for a compromise.

He had to know why she was after Gandalf. That was priority. Sure, it was a pretty solid secret, but there were a few people who could spill the beans. Nana, for one. A couple of hotel employees his parents might have bragged to?

His mind focused on practicalities, he was able to regain control of his body. Wanting to keep her in view, though, Dex strode through to the living room where he could still see Zoe from the front window.

Dex looked around the living room—bare walls and not a single framed photo to be found. Hell, that was the only thing that had changed since he'd lived here and his yearly school picture had graced the mantel. Nah, he probably didn't have to worry about his parents' bragging.

He glanced at Zoe, watching her back as she made her way through the gardens back to the hotel. The rich reds and golds of the leaves mimicked the streaks in her hair. Even bundled tightly against the cold, her hips still swayed to a tempting beat, enthralling him with their dance.

He was going to go for it. But he had to be cautious if he was going to play the game. Since it'd worked so well the first time, he was hauling out the costume again. He'd have to wait till tonight when it was dark, keep up the accent and be really, really careful. He was pretty sure he still had colored contact lenses up in his room. Leftovers from his role-playing days. He'd pop a pair in, make sure his one distinguishing feature was hidden. Just in case.

Excitement, more than just sexual, spiked in his gut. One way or another, he was going to win. His prize? The one he'd dreamed of for thirteen years.

Zoe Gaston.

6

GOD, SHE HATED being cold. In the spirit of sleuthing, she'd spent the afternoon and evening with some of her ex-classmates participating in a scavenger hunt. She'd been paired up with the puppy dog from the costume party, and they'd lost dismally, but she'd discovered that some of the people she'd gone to school with really weren't all that bad. Maybe because Heather, the puppy dog, couldn't stand Candice either. Zoe smiled. They'd had tons to talk about.

But Gandalf-talk? Everyone agreed that he was in their class. Speculation abounded but solid facts? Nada. It was like trying to find Batman.

Chilled through to the bone, she stomped her feet, trying to stir up some circulation as she attempted to fit the card key in its slot. She wasn't sure what made it worse, her shaking fingers or the fact that the hall light, an ornate sconce opposite her door, was burned out so the hallway was almost in darkness.

"Need help?"

Zoe gasped, spinning around and stabbing the plastic card out in front of her like a weapon.

Eyes huge, she sought, then found, the keeper of the deep, sweetly accented male voice. Her heart, already pounding, took off like a racehorse.

"You," she breathed. Excitement swirled through her

beneath a sudden attack of nervous caution. This was crazy. He was a stranger. Shouldn't she be careful?

He stepped through the shadows like a masked fantasy. He'd left off the cape this time, but was still wearing those thigh-hugging leather pants, soft cotton shirt and the mask.

Liquid heat seeped through her body, making her muscles lax, her brain soggy. It also made her nipples hard and pooled in damp desire between her legs. Oh, yeah, caution be damned.

It was the mask that turned her on the most. Maybe it was the air of danger it carried? Or—she sucked in her bottom lip and let her eyes slide over the planes of his cheekbones and jaw—maybe it was as simple as the sexy hero angle? Here was a guy who could sweep her off her feet, whisk her away and make all her fantasies come true.

Preferably before he flew off into the sunset this time.

"I'm not sure that you're quite up to fulfilling my needs, if you know what I mean," she pointed out with a little sniff. "If I recall, you left me hanging and quite unhelped last night."

"Why do I doubt you weren't able to take care of any frustrations I left you with all by yourself?" he murmured, a naughty smile tugging at a corner of his lush lips.

Zoe's own mouth twitched, but she refused to smile. She needed to keep in mind that, beneath her nerves, she was pissed at him.

"So, what? Do you provide batteries for all your hookups? You know, so they can relieve the sexual tension after you've left them all hot and bothered?"

He stepped closer. Close enough that she could almost make out his features in the darkened hallway. So close his scent filled Zoe's senses. She breathed in the subtle cologne, her mouth watering just a little for a taste of him.

"Were you hot and bothered?" he asked in a low, husky tone that sent a different kind of shiver through Zoe's body.

"Maybe warm and irritated," she shot back.

Her knees went weak when he grinned through the dark. Determined not to let him know, she cocked her hip to one side, tilted her chin and lifted a brow. She'd have pulled her shoulders back, too. But the move would have pressed her breasts against his chest and, damn it, he was going to have to work for that thrill. After all, he'd left her high and dry the night before.

Then he reached out and tucked a curl behind her ear, his fingers brushing against her cheek, and she damn near purred.

"Maybe I can get rid of that irritation?"

Irritation schmirritation. She'd get rid of anything he wanted her to for another taste of those lips.

"And the warmth?" she asked, her gaze locked on his mouth.

"I'm gonna heat that up to blazing hot," he told her as he leaned one hand against the wall behind her. He still didn't touch her, but the move made her feel deliciously trapped.

"And then?" she asked. She wanted nothing more than to let him, but some perverse part of her brain refused to let go of the insult of his leaving the night before.

"Did you want a play-by-play outline of my moves?" he asked, laughter dancing in his brown eyes. Something about his eyes nagged at Zoe for a second, but he moved, just a little, and her gaze dropped back to his grinning mouth.

"I guess I don't quite trust you," she admitted with a little shrug. The move brushed her shoulder against his forearm.

"Do you trust anyone?" he asked, a smile still curving his lips but his tone shrewd.

Unsure how to answer, Zoe pressed her lips together. Lying

was never a pretty thing. But admitting she couldn't trust was the equivalent to ripping off all her defenses and giving him a peek into her neurotic soul. Definitely not a sexy thing.

"Trust is earned," she finally said. Then she shot him a mischievous smile and suggested, "Maybe you should let me chain you to the bed until I have my way with you?"

He closed his eyes and let out a low groan, then shook his head and gave a rueful laugh. "You're killing me."

"Only with temptation."

With that in mind, she reached out and traced her palm over the hard muscles of his shoulder. The soft cotton of his shirt felt like silk beneath her hand as she smoothed over the hard muscles. Her nipples hardened at the delicious sensation, pressing against the tight constriction of her heavy winter coat. Suddenly Zoe felt so hot, she could strip naked and throw open the little window at the end of the hall and she knew she'd have steam coming off her body.

He took her hand and linked his fingers through hers. Holding it up to his mouth, he brushed those gorgeous lips over the backs of her knuckles, his breath tickling her flesh and making her wish she really were naked.

She rubbed her thumb over his lip. He grazed it with the edge of his teeth. Then, gently, he moved her hand to his against the wall, where he bracketed her wrist, holding her hand prisoner.

"No touching," he said. "Yet."

The *yet* sent a zing of desire spiraling through her body, catching her breath and spinning downward, deep into her belly and pooling damply between her legs.

"Now you're killing me," she said with a strained laugh.

"No. I want to know you better first. I promise I'll kiss you.

Touch you. But first I want to learn more. I want to know what will turn you on. What will drive you crazy. I want to customize everything I do with your pleasure in mind."

Zoe gave a helpless laugh. "Customize? You make it sound like a program or something."

He seemed to freeze for a second. Then he grinned, shaking it off so fast she wasn't sure if she'd imagined it. Before she could do more than narrow her eyes, he leaned his face close to hers. So close she could feel his breath caress her cheeks, the warm moisture of his mouth just millimeters from hers.

Zoe's breath froze in her chest. Her lids fell, her thick lashes tickling her cheeks before she forced her eyes open to meet his gaze. His eyes holding hers prisoner, he slowly ran his tongue over her bottom lip. Zoe moaned. He nipped gently, at the soft flesh. She almost came right then and there in intense, shocked pleasure.

"Tell me what you'd do to me," he said softly as he pulled back. Zoe leaned forward, trying to recapture his mouth. He gave a tiny shake of his head.

Zoe wanted to tell him to quit playing around and kiss her again. But a part of her was intrigued. There was something incredibly erotic about the idea of sexy talk. She'd always been more a girl of action than discussion, so this was virgin territory.

It was the word *virgin* that freed her inhibitions. Zoe had made it a point her entire adult life to avoid virginity in all things.

She tried to imagine what she'd do first.

"I'd strip you naked, of course," she told him.

Apparently needing to keep touching her, he used his free hand to twist one of her curls around his fingers, letting the silky strands slide in, then out of his grasp.

"I get to keep the mask," he told her, his mouth quirking in a one-sided grin.

"That's not fair."

"You can keep your boots on," he offered.

Zoe giggled. Then the image coalesced in her mind and the smile dropped from her lips. Oh, yeah. His gorgeous body spread over the silk coverlet. Her, straddling him wearing nothing but black, spiked boots.

Sexy.

Do-me-now sexy, as a matter of fact.

"Okay, you get the mask," she agreed breathlessly.

"Then what?"

Then she'd pin his hands over his head. With the mask to give them both a sense of forbidden freedom, she'd lean down and kiss him. She'd suck his tongue deep into her mouth like a lollipop, all the while holding his gaze so he got the message that she was going to do the same thing to his dick if he pleased her.

Mouth dry at the image, Zoe wet her lips. She'd never even had a dirty phone call. So the idea of verbalizing what she wanted—outside of bed, of course—was totally intimidating.

"Will you take charge?" he asked. "Or will you direct, telling me what to do to you?"

Despite the bizarre shyness seizing her vocal cords, Zoe forced herself to relax. "I'd kiss you," she told him. "But I'd kiss you in a way that drove you crazy."

"Since the sight of you naked except for those boots is guaranteed to drive me crazy, you wouldn't have far to go."

"I'd kiss your mouth," she told him, leaning her head back against the wall and letting her eyes drift to half-mast so she could better imagine the scenario. "I'd use my tongue, my teeth, until you groaned and begged me to touch you."

He let go of her hand to use his to unbutton the top button of her peacoat.

"I'm straddling you," she told him in a matter-of-fact tone that made his fingers still on her buttons before he leaned his forehead against hers, the cool fabric of his mask siphoning some of the warmth from her overheated body. It was then that Zoe realized the power, the intense sexual authority her words gave her over him.

Squirming a little, this time from desire and not embarrassment, Zoe let the fantasy loose in her mind.

"My knees are gripping your naked hips. I was holding your hands against the pillows, but when I sat up, I let them go. You reach up and touch my breasts."

Her nipples ached, pebbled and straining in need. Her breasts felt swollen. She imagined the feel of his hands cupping their heavy weight. The tips of his fingers swirling around her nipples, tweaking and flicking at the pointy tips.

It wasn't until a chill swept over her that Zoe realized he'd unbuttoned her coat all the way. She gave a little cry of delight as his hands slid under her sweater, tracing a cool trail along the sides of her waist until they reached her lacy bra.

"Tell me more," he urged, burying his mouth in the side of her throat. He inhaled deeply, then groaned and closed his fingers over her breasts. He didn't squeeze, didn't manipulate the aching flesh. He just waited.

Zoe's breath was coming in little pants now. She needed more. But, a tiny sane voice warned, she was standing in the hallway with a masked stranger.

"We need to—"

"Stop?" he asked.

"Get inside my room," she answered.

She felt his grin against her neck. Then, scraping his teeth over her sensitive flesh, he bit gently. Zoe gave a little keening moan, pressing her thighs together to intensify the wet, spiraling pressure between her legs.

"Key?"

Zoe forced her eyes open and tried to focus. What had she done with the key? She reluctantly moved, wishing he didn't ever have to stop working his magic on her throat, but wanting privacy even more. She saw the glint of white plastic out of the corner of her eye.

"I dropped it," she realized.

Before she could move, he bent down and grabbed it. But instead of straightening, he dropped to his knees and skimmed his hands over the back of her calves. Surprised, Zoe gave a little gasp. He smoothed his hands up her legs, curving them behind her knees. She shivered and closed her eyes to better savor the delight. If his hands felt this good through the thick denim of her jeans, how would they feel against her bare skin?

Then his hands cupped her butt and Zoe moaned. Encouraged, he leaned forward and, starting on her thigh, pressed tiny, openmouthed kisses up her leg. She held her breath. Would he? Eyes flying open, she shot an alarmed look down the hallway. It was deserted. She looked down and saw him watching her. Unable to tear her eyes away from the rich depths of his brown gaze, she stared. He gave a little grin, then pressed his mouth, hot and damp, against the crux of her legs. In response, wet heat flowed, dampening her panties.

"Wait," she said breathlessly. "Hold up."

He groaned. But he also held.

"Who are you?"

She felt rather than saw him freeze. Pull away.

And saw her orgasm flying out of her reach.

"Not who you are, exactly. I mean, I don't need a full name and background check. Sexual history would be nice, of course. All things considered that's just being smart, right? But nothing that would jeopardize your, um…" She was babbling. Zoe closed her eyes and took a deep, calming breath. Then she looked at him and gave a breathy laugh before shrugging. "You can keep your, you know, secret identity and all… Just, well, do we know each other?"

Zoe held her breath. It wasn't just the threat of losing what was promising to be one helluva sweet orgasm that she was worried about. It was the idea that this wasn't just a game to him. He was really determined to hide his identity. Why? Was he some creepy stalker who hung out at the inn, waiting to prey on single women? Even as the idea entered her head, she gave a mental eye roll. Right, because there were so many opportunities to run around in a mask without being questioned.

"We went to school together. I'm here with the reunion," he finally said. Then he frowned, the move wrinkling his mask over his forehead and giving him a slightly demonic look. "I'm not Brad, though."

Relief poured through her like champagne, complete with giddy bubbles of joy. Zoe gave a relieved giggle as the tension drained from her shoulders, leaving her arms limp at his waist. Until that second, she hadn't realized how worried she was. He was a former classmate, which put him firmly within groping limits.

Then his last words registered. Her eyes snapped open and she inspected as much of his face as she could.

She'd called him Brad last night. And five minutes later had been standing there alone and horny.

Bingo.

"I know you're not Brad," she said softly. Zoe licked her lips, realizing this was male ego territory. Fragile, sensitive and baffling. From what she'd heard from girlfriends, nothing guaranteed the end of promising sex faster than a misstep in this area. Personally, she'd never worried about a guy's ego before. Of course, no guy had ever acted jealous of her before. Unsure to play the game, she used her fallback. Blunt honesty. "I did think you were Brad last night. I mean, he's the only guy from our class who was ever interested in me. That and the camera guy said Brad was dressed up like a character from the same movie you are."

His words were so low, she had to lean in closer to hear them. "Brad wasn't the only guy interested in you."

Dex watched Zoe's mouth fall open.

"You don't have to say that," she said with a shake of her head that clearly told him she thought he was lying. "I'm already letting you in my room. It's not like sweet talk is going to get you kinky tricks or anything."

He snorted. Leave it to Zoe to take a silver lining and turn it into a noose. Not willing to let her tighten it around his neck, he got to his feet. On the way up, he was careful to let his body slide against hers. Damn, she felt good. Soft. He didn't want to blow his shot at feeling more of her. But he wasn't willing to let go of his point, either.

"Brad Young was a lot of things," he said, choosing his words as carefully as he chose his game plans. "But he wasn't known for his great discerning taste. He showed interest because he knew your crush would make you an easy mark."

He waited for her to lash out at him. Instead she raised both brows, then gave a slow nod. "Well, I guess that proves you really were in my class," she agreed.

Dex grinned.

"But nobody else was interested in me."

"Yeah. A few guys were. But you either intimidated them or were so focused on the football jock that you didn't notice."

"I never intimidated anyone," she argued, tossing her head so her curls danced around her face.

"Of course you did." Dex laughed. "You intimidated damn near everyone. From the lower classmen to the cheerleaders to the teachers."

Her smirk told him the thought of intimidating those people didn't much bother her. Then she tilted her head to one side and gave him a long look.

"Did I intimidate you?" she asked quietly.

Dex laughed and started to say no. Then he stopped. She'd been so smart. So damned sexy. Was that intimidation? If it wasn't, why hadn't he ever asked her out? He wanted to blame that on their friendship, but something about already deceiving her with the mask forced him to need be totally honest in all other ways. Uncomfortable, he shrugged. "I don't know that I'd quite say you intimidated me."

Her lips twitched as if she was going to laugh. Then she pursed them and raised a considering brow. Dex wondered if she was figuring him for a wimp.

"But you still had a thing for me?" Her tone was filled with doubt. The kind that told him nothing he said would make her believe him.

So he'd show her instead.

Dex stepped closer. Hard to do considering they were already toe to toe. The move pressed her lush breasts against his chest in a way that made him want to groan and give thanks. He scooped his hands into her hair, letting the silky waves wrap around his fingers.

Lowering his face, he let his mouth hover over hers, but he didn't touch. "I was crazy for you in the way dumb teenage boys are crazy. You inspired every dirty dream I'd ever had. You didn't look anything like the other girls in school. Or the girls on TV. Instead of being all fashion-doll perfect, you were edgy and just a little naughty."

Amusement flickered in her green eyes, dimming the doubts. Dex slid one hand from her hair to smooth the backs of his fingers over her soft cheek. He wanted to taste her lips again. To feel the warm wet heat of her kiss. But he forced himself to hold back.

"You wore ripped clothes that gave me a glimpse of your milky-white skin. I wanted to touch it, but figured you'd slap me away." Giving in just a little, he brushed his mouth over hers, sucking on her lower lip for just a second. Then, before he could get carried away, he pulled back.

"You took no crap from anyone. That attitude, pure confidence, made me want to do things I'd only heard about. Only thought about in the dark."

Unable to hold back anymore, Dex gave in to the clawing need and took her mouth in a deep, intense kiss. Tongues tangled, fighting for control. Teeth nipped, lips slid in a hot, wet dance of pleasure.

Needing more, his mouth still on hers, he reached behind her and slid the key card into the lock. Green light and he had the door open, her inside and two more steps and they were as close to heaven as they could get while clothed. In other words, horizontal on the bed.

"Is this where you keep your riding crop?" he asked, pulling back to look into her smiling face.

Zoe giggled.

"Crop or boots," she told him. "It's one or the other. You can't get greedy, after all."

"Boots, definitely." He slid a look over her body, barely visible in the dark room, baffled as only a guy could be. "But how do I get you naked and keep the boots?"

Her giggle turned to a sultry laugh. "All it takes is a little body English."

"Mine or yours?"

"Let's try yours first and see how it translates."

Figuring she knew how to strip herself better than he did, Dex turned himself over to the much more pleasurable prospect of enjoying her body. He rolled, so she was trapped beneath him. Instead of taking her mouth, this time he pressed soft, openmouthed kisses over her jaw, down her throat. He hummed as he reached the valley between her breasts, bared above her red sweater.

Temptation personified, Zoe writhed beneath him. Her thigh rubbed a sweet invitation against his straining dick. Dex could barely focus; she was driving him crazy. Grabbing desperately at control, he slid down farther, away from her thigh.

Zoe made a pouty sound in protest. Her hands curved over his shoulders, urging him upward.

So Dex went down.

Bunching her sweater in his hands, he pushed it up to bare her stomach. And groaned at the sight. A tiny red stone pierced her belly button, like a cherry on top of a very delicious treat.

Already as turned on as he thought he could get, Dex

closed his eyes and fought for control. Outflanked by desire, it spun just there, out of his reach.

He wanted the treat. And he wanted it now. Dex flicked the button of her jeans open, sliding the zipper down, then burying his face in her belly. He nipped gently at the soft flesh there, just beneath the glittery red stone. Then he slid lower.

"Off," he muttered.

She almost killed him complying. She lifted her hips, bringing the juncture of her jeans right up to his mouth. Ignoring whatever she was doing with the rest of the fabric, Dex buried his face there with a growl. He could smell her, female and inviting. He needed to taste her.

As soon as the denim cleared her hips, Dex dove in. He cupped his hands over the bare skin of her butt so she couldn't lie flat again. She gasped, then moaned as he followed the path of her pants by kissing his way down her leg. At her knees, the jeans bunched. Dex slid to the edge of the bed, slipped her boots off, then grabbed the hems of the pants and pulled them and her silky red undies off. Then he stared.

"Damn," he breathed. "You're incredible."

She lay there, her hair a tousled tangle of colors around her face. A flush, desire he knew, since she didn't blush, washed her cheeks with soft color. Her eyes were slumberous and challenging at the same time. Daring him to pleasure her. Begging him to do it soon.

His eyes trailed down her body. Her breasts quivered temptingly with each rapid breath. He wanted to yank the sweater off her to see them. Were they as round and heavy as they looked? Were her nipples dark or light? Large or small? He couldn't believe he was going to find out.

But first… He slid his gaze lower, to the dark triangle of tidy curls between her legs. He ran his finger over her thigh, just there where it met her hips. Her skin was like silk.

Forcing himself away from the temptation beneath those curls, he slid his palms over her thighs, giving a low growl at how smooth and warm her skin was. He gently traced the back of her knees, his mouth quirking to one side when she giggled helplessly. His fingers traced a pattern over her calves until he reached his objective.

The boots.

He cupped both her ankles in his hands. The leather beneath his fingers was a major turn-on. Was this a newly discovered kink? Did he care?

Dex stood at the foot of the bed, still holding her boot-clad feet in his hands. He stared down the tempting length of her body and heaved a huge, shaky sigh. Heaven. She was pure heaven. And he was the lucky man about to get himself a tiny piece of that heaven.

Dex released one of her legs. She settled it, knee raised, on the bed. He lifted the other to his mouth, pressing a hot, openmouthed kiss just above her boot. He kissed his way up her calf. When he reached her knee, he dropped to his own between her legs, then slid down flat between her thighs.

Using his tongue, he traced a pattern up the inside of her thigh. He looked up. Great view. His already rigid erection throbbed at the sight of her damp, glistening pink lips.

Never a man to savor when he was starved for the feast, Dex had to force himself to go slow. He draped her legs over his shoulders to lift her to the perfect kissing height. He breathed in. Her scent filled his mind, making his mouth water. He traced his fingers over the swollen flesh. Zoe mewed a tiny sound of approval. His heart pounded, excitement and anticipation swirling in his head. Finally, he gave in. With his tongue, he teased and tasted. A little sip here, a tiny nibble there, he took his time.

And if the impatient fingers tightening in his hair and the low moans were any indication, he was driving Zoe just as crazy as he felt.

His tongue swirled, probed, stabbed. Her moans grew shorter, in time with her panting breath.

His hands found the soft curves of her breasts under the warmth of her sweater. He did no more than curve his fingers over the lace-covered mounds, squeezing in time with his darting tongue.

Zoe's thighs tightened on his shoulders, her body stiffening as she raised her hips closer to his mouth. Dex slid one hand back down, working her swollen nub with his tongue while he used one finger, then two, to send her over the edge.

Zoe's pants took on a keening edge. Her fingers gripped his hair. He sucked the tasty flesh into his mouth.

She exploded.

The sound of her satisfaction rang out, filling his ears. Filling his heart. Dex slowed the movement of his tongue, soothing now instead of tormenting.

His own breath coming in gasps, Dex eased back to watch her come down from her orgasm. Face flushed, eyes closed, she looked like every dream he'd ever had. If his hands weren't full, he'd pinch himself to see if this was real.

Yeah, this was a tiny taste of heaven, all right. And it was even better—Zoe was even better—than he'd dared imagine.

He shuddered with pleasure as he watched her. Images flashed through his mind, a snapshot of this moment imprinting itself in his brain. Oh, yeah, this was heaven. And just as soon as he caught his breath, he was going to get an even bigger taste.

7

AT FIRST, Dex thought the vibration in his thigh was sexual arousal reaching a never-before-felt fever pitch. Then he realized it was his BlackBerry buzzing.

His groan had nothing to do with pleasure. He wanted to ignore it. To continue to focus on what was important: sinking into the glorious oblivion of Zoe's body.

But his phone would only buzz if Tony, the hotel manager, had an emergency.

Damn.

"I have to go," he murmured against the silken skin of Zoe's stomach.

"You mean you have to come," she said, her fingers smoothing over his shoulders in a comforting, kneading motion. Despite his aching frustration, Dex smiled. All she needed was a purr and she'd be the epitome of a satisfied kitty cat.

He forced himself to raise his head from the soft warmth of her body and meet her eyes in the dim light. Their dark-green depths showed contentment, a look he'd rarely seen on Zoe. Oh, yeah, sexual awareness was definitely still there. But like a smoldering fire, the flames were banked for the moment.

Dex's body screamed in protest, his throbbing dick begging for the pleasure Zoe's eyes promised. His heart, up till now just an organ, called out its own protest. He'd finally connected with the woman he'd spent most of his life dreaming about. Lying there, engulfed in her warmth and sweetness, Dex realized how vital Zoe was to him, whether she was actually in his life or not. But now that he'd had her there, so to speak, he was damned sure going to make sure she stayed in it.

Desire made it hard to strategize, but Dex's brain was already compiling ideas. Ways to hold on to Zoe. Then his phone buzzed again. Responsibility fought with need as he ground his teeth. He was going to kill Tony.

"I really, really want to stay here and come with you," he said with an apologetic look. Knowing there was no easy way to do it, he sucked in a breath and pushed away from her body. The rich musky aroma of her satisfaction filled his senses in mocking torment. "I really have to go. I'm…" He didn't want to sound all mysterious, but he couldn't admit he had to run downstairs and see what the emergency was. "I'm needed."

Her lips quirked. "Did you get a secret message?"

He stood, his phone only adding to the pressure of his too-tight pants. "You could put it that way."

Realizing he wasn't joking, Zoe sat up and, as if she suddenly remembered she was only wearing her sweater and a very sexy pair of boots, she tugged the red knitted fabric low on her hips.

"You're serious? You're leaving me? Again?"

The WTF tone warned him if he ever again wanted to taste the pleasure that still lingered on his tongue, he'd better talk damned fast.

"I am," he admitted. Before she could hiss like the cat he'd just compared her to, he leaned over and took her mouth with his. Lips melted together, tongues tangling in a dance that made him curse the unforgiving lack of give in leather and shift uncomfortably as his erection threatened to cut off circulation to his legs.

Thankfully, Zoe didn't bite but gave herself over to the kiss, rising up to her knees to press her body against him. Dex wrapped his arms around her, his hands smoothing over her back under her sweater.

His leg buzzed again.

Pressed against him as she was, Zoe felt the zing. She pulled her mouth from his and leaned her head back, her eyes narrowed.

"You really are getting a message? Or is that an alarm that warns you that you'll turn into a pumpkin if you don't hurry away?"

"More like some stupid work I'd promised to do," he muttered, glad for the mask because he was sure he was blushing. God, he finally got the woman of his dreams naked and his pants kept vibrating, forcing him to give her up to take care of work for his daddy. Talk about a twisted Oedipal issue.

He couldn't figure out the look she was giving him. Like she was measuring. Which would be great, if he had his pants off. But not when the appraisal was over something other than the sexual prowess he'd been hoping to impress her with. Or at least press into her.

"Do you always keep your promises?" Zoe asked, giving him a seductive look through her lashes. Her fingers did a slow, tempting dance up his chest, making it hard to focus on anything but how good she made him feel.

"Of course," he said once her words sank into his brain. He might hide his identity, use a mask to seduce the woman of his dreams and sidestep any direct questions regarding his career. But he did keep his promises.

"Then if I asked you if we could finish what we started here, would you promise me we would?"

Dex was sure weeping in gratitude would negate the manliness of the warrior persona. Of course, the mask and leather pants had probably already chipped away at it a little so he wasn't willing to take any risks.

Instead, he grinned and brushed a featherlight kiss over the tip of her nose, then stepped away in fine superhero fashion. If he'd been wearing the cape, he'd have swirled it around him.

"For you, anything," he vowed, taking her hand in his and raising it to his lips. Zoe giggled, obviously enjoying his campiness. He bowed low over her hand, then turned it over and pressed a moist kiss to the center of her palm.

"And…" She hesitated, then with a deep breath rushed on. "Will you tell me who you are? Before this week is over, will you reveal yourself, so to speak?"

The intensity of his fear of her rejection slammed into him like a brick wall. Painful, damaging misery. But how could he deny her? "If you'll trust me, then, yes, I promise I'll tell you before the end of the week. But…I want this time. Is that okay?"

In other words, he was a chicken-shit procrastinator. But that sounded so unromantic. He watched her consider his request, her eyes thoughtful, her delicious mouth pursed. Then she nodded and he felt the weight of the world drop from his shoulders.

"Throw in an extra climax or two, let me be on top, and you're on," she negotiated with a wicked grin. Delight danced in her eyes though color washed gently over her chest as if she wasn't used to the sexy talk, and felt a little embarrassed.

"I promise," Dex said, meaning it. His mind was already

racing with ways to make their next rendezvous the most incredibly, romance-novel-sexy encounter of her life.

And next time, he might even get to take his pants off.

ZOE RODE THE ELEVATOR down to the hotel lobby the next morning grinning in satisfaction. Nothing like a couple of orgasms to relax a girl and put her in a chipper mood.

Her body felt loose and limber, as if she'd just had a long, intense Hatha yoga session. Or a sexy guy in a mask go down on her. Given the choices, she couldn't wait to get the masked hunk out of his mask. And everything else.

She deliberately focused on her body's residual pleasure and not on the vestiges of suspicious frustration nagging in the back of her mind. Hey, she'd got hers, she reminded herself. There was no reason to think the hottie with the magic tongue was trying to take advantage of her. But she still wanted, needed, to know who was beneath that mask.

She tapped her fingers against her hip as she wondered what he had to gain. Then she shook her head and forced herself to stop. Nope. He'd asked her to trust him. It would have been easier if he'd asked her to run naked through the lobby while turning cartwheels and singing the school fight song. But she was going to give it a shot. After all, she'd be damned if she'd ruin the best sex of her life with her fallback mode of mistrust.

Her smile back in place, she sauntered through the lobby as though she was still wearing leather and a riding crop. In command, sure of her own sexuality. It felt damned good.

Heads turned as she walked past. Brows arched, elbows nudged. Zoe knew she was being watched, whispered about. She didn't give a damn.

She smirked at herself. How many times had she told herself that in her life? Millions, for sure. But this time, she one-hundred-percent meant it. The difference between meaning and pretending was like the difference between a Wal-Mart knockoff and Prada. Totally awesome.

Starved after her little physical exertion and unable to stay in her room for fear of going crazy replaying the sexual encounter over and over in her head, Zoe wanted a late-morning snack.

With that in mind, she headed toward the restaurant. Halfway there, she heard someone called her name. For a brief second, she debated pretending she didn't hear. After all, she might not care that anyone was gossiping about her, but that didn't mean she wanted it in her face while she was eating her pie.

Then she sighed and, not bothering to hide her impatience, turned to see who was hailing her. She watched one of the red-headed twins, she couldn't tell if it was Jingle or Jangle, teetering her way on spiked heels.

She should have kept going.

"Zoe, there you are," the woman said. Once she got closer, the stylized Julie written on her necklace cleared up the identity issue. But not Zoe's desire to run. "I've been hoping to see you. We should chat, hmm?"

"Why?" Zoe asked bluntly.

"Oh, all kinds of reasons." Julie's eyes turned a little brittle, but her smile didn't drop away. "Reunion business, old times. Some dirt on Brad Young, if you're interested. A shot at paying Candy back for being such a bitch to you yesterday…"

Zoe arched a brow. She didn't care about anything except the dirt on Brad. And then only if that dirt had to do with his job.

But she knew the game. It was the whole enchilada or nothing, so she'd have to play nice to get the one piece of info she wanted.

"I was just getting something to eat," Zoe said, poking her thumb over her shoulder toward the restaurant. "C'mon."

Not the most gracious invitation, but Julie obviously didn't care. She sent a snide look at a few of the gawkers, lifted her sculpted chin in the air and stepped in time with Zoe to the restaurant. From the whispers that followed them, Zoe surmised that Candice had already started stirring up gossip and Julie wasn't doing herself any favors by hanging out with the geeky Goth-girl.

Irritated despite herself, Zoe pretty much ignored Julie until they'd been served tea and pie. Once the waiter set the slice of dutch apple in front of her, Zoe scooped up a bite, humming her pleasure. She looked at the redhead sitting across from her nursing a very unappetizing-looking piece of sugar-free chocolate cream.

If that was the price of popularity, Zoe would stick with her dutch apple.

"So, what's up?" Zoe asked.

"Like I said, I wanted a chance to chitchat. You know how these reunions go. Everyone going every which way, all the events so planned and organized. It's hard to find time to sit and talk about old times."

Zoe took another bite, savoring the cinnamon richness as she contemplated the pretty redhead's words.

"So you want info and figured cornering me would get you an exclusive? Or at least a head start on whoever else is up for the crown of reunion gossip queen?"

She waited for the snarl. But Julie surprised her. Instead of getting ugly, she just smiled. A genuine smile. The kind that crinkled the skin around her blue eyes and made her look like a real person, not a made-up doll.

"I always remembered you as clever, but I must have missed the blunt element of your personality," Julie said, taking a bite of her own pie.

"Since I can barely recall more than three encounters between us in the three years of school, I doubt you noticed any of my more charming personality traits."

Julie smirked. Then she set her fork down and leaned forward, her elbows planted on the table. "I think I like you," she said.

Zoe didn't know what she thought about that declaration. She knew she should sneer, but her heart warmed a little at the words. What was the other woman after? Instead of asking, she took another bite of spiced apples and waited.

"Look, I'm curious. Maybe we didn't hang out in school, but I do remember you. And from what I recall, you weren't exactly Little Miss School Spirit. I'm surprised you came to the reunion."

"Was there a level of spirit required to revisit old times?"

"No, but the general recollection is that you hated old times."

Aha. "General recollection? Translation, the gossip mill?"

Julie's lips quirked and she pressed her coral fingernail to the tip of her nose.

"I guess it wouldn't be too far of a stretch to say that I wasn't fond of old times," Zoe mused. Then she shrugged. "But that was then. This is now. And I'm here at the reunion. Defies logic, doesn't it?"

"That it does. But I'm betting there's a reason you came back. And I figured that maybe that's where we could help each other out."

Zoe gave her empty plate a sad look. She should have

eaten more slowly. She had a feeling it would have been wise to have something to do with her mouth for the next few minutes.

"Why would you want to help me out?" Sans pastry, she wanted this conversation over with as fast as possible. She felt weird sitting here talking like girly buddies with someone she'd actively mocked for years. The realization that Julie wasn't a total snotty, humorless bitch wasn't sitting too well with her pie. "And why would I want to let you?"

"First off, you must have come back for a reason. I have an idea what that reason is, and I'd be happy to help you. Why?" she asked before Zoe could. "Because you're my best shot at getting what *I* want this week."

Zoe waited.

"You're trying to find someone, right? Someone named Gandalf?"

"Do you know who it is?" Zoe asked, leaning closer and holding her breath.

"Not yet, but I can help you find out."

Zoe considered the offer. Julie probably was her best bet. And what did she have to lose? So she told the redhead the basics.

"Computer games?" Julie pursed her lips and considered. "A few people come to mine. Brad, of course. But he's more the sports type than the fantasy type."

Zoe nodded in agreement.

"Teresa Roberts is rumored to own some kind of computer company. There might be a couple of others, too. I'll ask around. Maybe the art teacher, Mrs. Greenberg, will have an idea. Whoever it is had to be a pretty good artist, right?"

Zoe nodded her gratitude, then asked, "And in return?"

"I want to beat Candice to the reunion crown," Julie admitted.

Zoe grinned. "Works for me," she said before she could help herself.

Julie gave a tiny frown and tilted her head. "You're sure? I mean, her theory is you came back to get it for yourself."

"Candice has a theory about me?"

"Candice has a theory about everything and everybody."

"Do tell...?" Zoe leaned her own elbow on the table and cupped her chin, her eyes round, brows raised.

Julie's lips twitched.

"Let's see... According to Candice's theory, you're here for revenge, aka the crown. Most of the other women are here to see if she got fat, the men to see if they can get lucky. I'm sucking up for a job connection." The redhead paused to catch her breath and roll her eyes. "My sister is looking for a husband. Brad Young is getting ready to invest a pile of money in some video business. And Mr. Lee is hoping for student recommendations to snag himself a raise."

Zoe grinned. Bingo. It was all she could do to keep her ass in the seat instead of jumping up to do a happy dance. If Candice was right, Brad *was* the video-game wizard.

"Well, we've already debunked her theory on me. D'ya think any of her others have any weight?" After all, Candice might be faulty.

Julie shrugged. "Candice is usually fifty-fifty in the theory department. She's good at gossip gathering, but lousy at factoring in the people dynamic."

"Unlike you?"

"Precisely. And my people skills tell me that while you're not interested in the crown yourself, you might be willing to help me get it away from Candice. Especially if it doesn't take much effort on your part."

Zoe couldn't help it, she laughed out loud. "So according to your people skills, I'm all about revenge, but kinda on the lazy side?"

Julie got a horrified look in her eyes, then she gave a sheepish shrug and said, "Well, yeah."

"Okay," Zoe agreed as her laughter trailed off. "That's close enough. What do you want me to do?"

Julie gave a little whoop, then ducked her shoulders and looked around to see if anyone had noticed. Paling, she grimaced and slunk low in her chair. Zoe looked over her shoulder and saw Candice following the hostess to a table across the room.

"Busted?" she asked, her tone mocking to hide her surprising hurt. Well, well. Rejection once again.

"Nah. It's not like our sitting together won't get back to her. But I don't want a confrontation yet," Julie muttered, sounding like she was having the time of her life. "She's holding a rah-rah meeting, trying to get people to sign up for her public relations services. She sees this reunion as an extended nag-fest. But, you know, in the spirit of surprise making her defeat all the sweeter, I'm going to sneak out of here before she sees me. And, well, I'd rather keep our little plan between us for a while."

"She's really in public relations?" Zoe asked before Julie could get up, eyeing the obvious strong-arm tactics of the blonde and wondering if she managed to get any repeat business.

"Temporarily," Julie verified. "For all her rubbing her perfection in our faces, I don't think she's happy. All she talks about is her big life goal. Marry rich. I'm pretty sure she sees the reunion as her ticket there, too."

Zoe sent Candice a long, curious look. She'd always figured the blonde was on top of the world.

"Sounds kinda…"

"Pitiful?" Julie gave her an amused look as she tried to slide out of the chair without standing. "Don't feel bad for her. She's telling anyone who'll listen that she's got Brad on the hook and that he has some hush-hush job that apparently pays beaucoup bucks. Candy's good at looking out for herself. But I've got to go. We can talk somewhere else, huh?"

Julie gave a little hurry-up motion with her hand. Zoe snickered and shook her head. This would be one of the reasons why she'd never made it in the popular circles. She didn't have the mind—or the patience—for this kind of intrigue. Zoe didn't care about the contest between Julie and Candice, but she did care about Brad's hush-hush job. Another link to Gandalf.

"I'm going to walk off my pie," she told the redhead with a friendly smile. "You catch up to me later and fill me in on the crown conspiracy deets, okay? In exchange, I want all the information you can gather on that job of Brad's."

Zoe paused and considered. Julie, being the master of gossip, was the best person to ask. But more important, she might have a clue about who had dressed up as Aragorn and given Zoe such a mind-blowing orgasm last night. "I'd also be interested in a list of who dressed up as what. I cut out of the party early and am trying to figure out who came in one particular costume."

Julie gave her an intrigued look, as though she was going to ask for details. Then Candice's laugh washed over them like tiny shards of broken glass and, with a little shudder, she nodded. Then, glancing quickly over her shoulder to see if it was safe, she slid out of her chair. She tossed a ten on the table and hurried away.

Watching her go, Zoe's feelings tangled in confusion. She couldn't blame the gal for wanting to grab the crown from Candice's perfectly coifed head. But did Zoe want to end up in the middle of a bitch fight?

Zoe stood to leave, glancing over at Candice holding court. The other woman met her eyes, a sneer curling her bubble-gum-pink lips.

Zoe returned the sneer with a cheery finger wave. Bitch fight, smitch fight. She had a new friend and she was going to help her win. Because, despite knowing Julie was using her to get back at Candice, Zoe felt the offer of friendship was real.

A warm feeling of belonging Zoe had never had in school wrapped around her. Damn, she felt good. Free, even. She sauntered out of the restaurant with a grin on her face. Her smile grew bigger as she entered the lobby and saw Brad. Perfect.

She called out his name. Her words were drowned by the chorus of men calling to him, though. A few shoulder slaps and loud greetings later and the group of a half-dozen guys headed for the small lounge.

Zoe considered following, then saw Dex meet them at the lounge door. She frowned. She'd forgotten that while he wasn't a card-carrying member of the jerk club, he was a fringe visitor.

She considered. Should she follow them? Before she could decide, a tiny voice spoke from somewhere around her elbow.

"Hello, sweetie. How about a cup of tea and some cards?"

Startled, Zoe turned and saw Dex's grandma. Her automatic smile took on a wicked edge. "Mrs. Drake, I'd love to have tea with you. I need some advice."

"SO WHAT'S THIS WEEK'S bet? Which babe do I have to do to win?"

Dex silently groaned and wished he could be anywhere but in the lounge with these yahoos. But it had seemed smart to fall right back into the pattern of tagging along. Not for their company—he'd be hard-pressed to find a bigger bunch of jerks—but for information. The only way to know what Brad Young was up to was to be in his inner circle. And since Brad was usually up to no good, and that no good might involve Zoe, Dex had learned long ago to grit his teeth and keep a blank face, both when he heard the crap spewed, and later when he'd secretly ruined the jerks' plans.

"But this time you guys need to make the bet a little sweeter," Brad continued. "What was it last time? A C-note from each of you?"

"How about the keys to my '66 Mustang?" AJ Maddox, balding ex-quarterback, challenged.

"You'd never hand those keys over," Brad said as he popped open another beer.

"I would if you actually get her to go all the way."

Brad stopped laughing and lowered his beer.

"One hundred bucks from each of you, plus you kick in your keys?" Brad clarified.

"But only if you actually do her. No getting her half-naked then freaking out when your parents show up like you did ten years ago."

"When the hell did they start going to the drive-in?" Brad muttered, drinking to hide his embarrassment over his last failed attempt at Zoe, and the reason behind it.

Out of practice, a smirk slipped off Dex's lips before he blanked his expression. That drive-in bust had been one of his triumphs of revenge. Scoring two tickets for Brad's parents in a faux radio-show prize had been brilliant. They'd ruined Brad's date with Zoe, which was his plan. What he hadn't counted on, unfortunately, had been Brad's humiliation the next week at school. In retaliation, the jerk had dubbed Zoe the girl most likely to die a virgin and made her cry. As much as Dex knew it was Brad's fault, he'd always felt guilty about his role in hurting Zoe.

Which was just one more thing he wanted to make Brad Young pay for.

"Deal?" AJ asked.

"It'll be interesting to see if you can handle a gal who carries her own whip," one guy threw in.

"Sweet." Brad's grin spread, huge and dirty. Dex wanted to pound his fist into the wall. Even more, he wanted to pound all the assholes gathered in the lounge a few times. Struggling to calm down, he tried reason first.

"I can't believe you guys are still doing that betting thing," Dex said in an offhand, jovial tone. His look conveyed the same impression as if he'd said he couldn't believe they were still doing homework and keeping curfew.

"It's good times," Brad said with a shrug. "Everyone still likes to play, old buddy. Except you, I suppose. Still not willing to bet with us?"

Irritation was clear in Brad's overly affable smile. The other guy had always been frustrated that Dex had caught on to his game and closed up his wallet. It wasn't the football player's brains or skills that had really made him a leader in school. It was because, one way or another, everyone owed him something—everyone except Dex.

"Nah, I'm not a betting guy," Dex said. He grabbed a

bottled water and let himself enjoy Brad's annoyance as he untwisted the top.

"Once a chicken, always a chicken," Brad taunted.

"Is this where we all pull them out and compare?" Dex joked. Brad shut up when the other guys laughed, but a shrewd look settled on his face. Dex realized he probably should have played it a little mellower, but years of calling his own shots had ruined his ability to play beta to anyone.

"It's all harmless fun. And hey, the girls always thank me for their part in these bets," Brad bragged.

"Why don't you set your sights on another cutie this round?" Dex suggested easily. His smile was affable, his words casual. "You're still big dude on campus. Why not chase down one of the gals you're always saying are so hot for you?"

"I say Zoe Gaston's hot for me. And I'm gonna win the bet." Brad gave him a mocking smile, one that clearly said this was his way of drawing the line in the sand. As he smiled, he stepped forward, fists clenched and shoulders pulled back menacingly.

Fight? Hell, yeah. Nobody was screwing around with Zoe. Not this time around.

Dex curled his fist tight. Screw this. Years of frustration, irritated competition and this asshole winning Zoe without Dex even having a chance to step up to the plate boiled over. Before he could swing, a husky, oh-too-familiar voice called out a greeting.

"Gentlemen."

8

THEY ALL JUMPED. Adrenaline surging like an electrical storm, Dex forced himself to relax his fingers. One last glare at Brad and he turned slowly to see Zoe standing in the lounge's double glass doors, a bright smile on her face and a few bags of chips in her arms.

Her smile dimmed, a crease settling between her eyes when she got hit by the tension in the room.

What the hell was she doing here? Was Brad right? The green-eyed monster blurred his vision for a second as he shot a calculating look between the two of them. Was she still chasing the jerk? Wasn't Dex, albeit in his masked form, enough for her? Zoe's gaze flicked between the two men, her frown deepening. Then, as if realizing every set of eyes in the room were pinned on her, she wiped her expression clean and held up the snacks.

"I heard you were partying in here and needed something to go with the beer."

"Great timing," Brad said in a jolly tone. "Dex and I were just talking about you."

"Really?" she asked slowly, her tone as suspicious as the look she shot Dex. "Care to share the details?"

"Just talking about what a great reunion queen you'll make," Brad said with an evil glance at Dex.

"Right," Zoe said, her sarcastic tone making Dex grin for the first time since he'd walked in.

Brad started to sling compliments at Zoe, but she just stared at him as though he was a science puzzle she was trying to work her way through.

"What'd you come in here for, again?" Dex interrupted, not caring that he was being rude. He wanted to leave and he wanted Zoe with him.

She narrowed her eyes, then indicated the snacks. "I ran into your grandmother in the lobby. She said she was delivering these, but needed to take care of something. I told her I'd bring them in."

Dex frowned. He'd thought his grandmother was safely tucked away at her weekly Reiki session. No matter. He strode forward, took the bags of chips from Zoe and tossed them at Brad and his buddies. Jocks that they were, they caught each one. Even though Brad's was aimed directly between his eyes.

"Enjoy," Dex said. "The room is yours for the next hour, compliments of Drake Inn."

With that, he pressed his hand to the small of Zoe's back in unspoken command.

And was damned grateful when she only shot him a snotty look and didn't take a swipe at him. He guided her from the room, his hand sliding from the gentle arch of the small of her back to the curve of her hip. He felt her catch her breath. She slanted him a sideways glance but didn't slow down. Dex was glad. He knew he should be more careful, but he just didn't give a damn anymore. Because as good as slapping a sign on her back, he knew Brad caught his message.

Zoe was his.

ZOE NEEDED A LIFE preserver. Something to keep her safe while she rode the waves of the leftover undercurrents buffeting through the room.

She arched a brow in question, but Dex ignored her. Instead, he just jerked his chin toward the door, indicating that he was leaving and if she wanted to go, she'd better keep her ass up.

She wanted to tell him to hang on. To insist he fill her in on the scene she'd walked in on. Why were he and Brad going nose to nose? What was with the testosterone overload? She'd felt like a meaty bone in there, standing between two growling dogs. And here she was, waltzing out with apparently the biggest dog of the two. Since the other dog was most likely Gandalf, she really should have stood her ground and waited to talk to Brad. But Dex had bared his macho teeth, laid his hand on her and she'd just sort of melted.

She should be worrying about her priorities here, but all she cared about was when the hell had Dex turned all sexy and powerful?

"What's my grandma taking care of?" Dex asked, sounding as though he didn't really care but had to say something to break the ice.

"She's searching for wedding tiara patterns to bead my headpiece," Zoe said casually, giving him a bland look. Dex almost tripped over his feet, his gaze flying to her face so fast his eyeballs probably had whiplash. She took a deep, slightly evil sort of pleasure in his reaction.

"You're getting married?" His tone was a combination of shock and protest. Zoe smiled serenely and kept walking.

Finally getting his feet back under him, Dex hurried to catch up with her halfway across the lobby.

"Why is my grandmother beading you a headpiece?" he

asked, laying his hand on her arm to stop her forward momentum. Zoe's breath stuck in her throat at his touch. A fission of energy zinged up her arm, tingled down her body and curled her toes.

"It was so cool to see her again," Zoe said, sidestepping his question. "She's really looking great."

Something niggled in the back of her mind as her gaze traced the lines of his jaw and the full temptation of his mouth.

What was wrong with her? She was turning into a total trampy get-around girl. All she could think about, looking at Dex, was how it'd feel to have that gorgeous mouth on her body, just as she'd had the masked hunk's on her last night. Was it the altitude that had her wanting to do sexy times with every man she saw here? She recalled the jerk brigade and Brad, looking like a puffed-up kid who'd been told he was losing his favorite toy. At least she wasn't getting hot and bothered over *every* guy. Just her ex-best friend and a costumed stranger.

A costumed stranger who'd driven her to a panting orgasm with his wicked tongue play the night before. Conflict knotted in Zoe's stomach. She should be focusing on him, shouldn't she? Instead of her best friend. A guy who was sweet and upright and, well, long-term.

Finally, her usual mantra surfaced. She might be at this reunion for the duration to help her brother. But that's as long as her attention span lasted. When in doubt, believe in the short-term. Nothing lasted. She'd seen that over and over in life. So depending on anyone or anything other than herself was crazy. Which meant she owed it to her old friend to bury her lust instead of flirting her way to a promise she wouldn't keep. Which really sucked.

"Zoe?" Dex placed a hand on her arm, pulling them both to a stop.

"Huh?"

Dex frowned, his brilliant turquoise eyes dark with impatience. "Who are you marrying?"

Should she laugh or cry at the irony of talking marriage with the sweetest guy she'd ever had the hots for when that exact topic made him completely off-limits? If she couldn't stick it out with a job because she was sure once people got to know her, really know her, they'd bail, how impossible did that make a forever commitment? She'd never really cared. Until now. Despite the sadness in her chest, her lips twitched at the look on Dex's face.

"You, apparently."

She used his shock to pull free and continue her way across the lobby. As she expected, he caught up with her at the doors to the garden.

"Care to share the details?" he asked in a matter-of-fact tone that did nothing to hide his amused shock. He pushed the door open for her. Zoe had to brush against his body to get through what seemed to be a deliberately narrow opening. "I don't recall the proposal."

Zoe shivered a little. Telling herself it was the chilly afternoon air and not depression over what would never be, she stepped onto the cobblestone path. *Get over it,* she warned herself.

As soon as Dex joined her, she gave him a teasing smile and shrugged. "It's not coming for a few months, I hear. Apparently, once it does we'll be well on our way to happy ever after, a big business deal, four kids, if you can believe it, and a wild sex life. I have to say, the details on that last one would have been extremely intriguing if they hadn't been coming from your sweet little ol' grandma."

She had to give him credit. His shock didn't last nearly as long as hers had. Other than that, she'd have to say they were both equally amused, but Dex's cheeks did sport a tinge of color she was betting wasn't due to the wind-chill factor.

"Tarot cards?" he asked with a roll of his eyes.

"Yep. Who knew such innocuous pieces of paper could sport so many naked bodies?"

Dex snorted. "My grandmother claims the nudity inspires her psychic senses or something like that."

"Well she was inspired big-time, let me tell you." Zoe wasn't sure what had been worse. Shock or embarrassment. And she'd had plenty of both to compare from the moment that sweet white-haired lady had dragged her over to a small damask-covered table in the corner of the lobby. Once she'd pulled out those gilt-edged cards filled with compelling—albeit mostly naked—images, Zoe had felt like Alice down the rabbit hole. Then the octogenarian had started describing sex between Zoe and her only grandson. *Surreal* didn't begin to describe her reaction.

Dex leaned around, peering at her face as they walked. "She embarrassed you?"

"I wouldn't say that," Zoe lied, tucking her hands into the front pockets of her jeans to keep her fingers warm. All she'd wanted was to ask the older woman if she'd heard of Gandalf. As soon as she'd tried, though, Mrs. Drake had said all answers were in the cards and whipped out those naked pictures. Definitely not the answers Zoe had been looking for.

"She did. You never blush, but you do get this wrinkle between your eyes when you're embarrassed." He leaned closer, practically bending in half to walk by her side and still look into her face. "Yep, there it is. That cute little crease."

He thought she was cute? Nonplussed, Zoe didn't know what to say. After their encounter over breakfast, she'd wondered. Sure, he'd said she looked great, but that was one of those typical things to say when they see each other again. But cute? That was, like, special.

Wasn't it? And how pathetic did it make her to get all giddy and schoolgirl-excited at the idea?

"I wasn't embarrassed, really," she prevaricated. "I do admit I was a little shocked to hear your grandma's take on your sexual preferences, though."

Instead of blushing, Dex just laughed. A deep, sexy belly laugh that made Zoe grin in delight. Well, well. So her geek-turned-sexy-as-hell old friend wasn't that shy after all. Nor a prude if the wicked glint in his eyes was any indication.

"You'll have to fill me in on the details. Grandma's pretty imaginative. I might pick up a few tips from her reading, huh?"

Zoe thought of the varied likes and dislikes the old lady had listed. She still didn't know how she'd gotten stilettos, whipped cream and outdoor play from those random cup-and-stick covered cards. But the idea of those and Dex combined nicely in Zoe's mind. Oh, yeah, she'd like to cover him in whipped cream, wrap her stiletto-clad feet around his hips and ride him like a wild stallion under the full moon.

She gulped, trembling a little at the rush of desire washing over her.

"We should go back in," Dex said all of a sudden.

Zoe frowned, her gaze flying to his face in consternation. That mumbo-jumbo psychic thing didn't run in the family, did it? Had he just read her dirty mind and decided to run?

"Why?" she asked baldly.

"You're shivering," he pointed out.

Relief poured through Zoe at the same time she clued in that she was freezing in her light sweater.

"No kidding? I forgot how damned cold autumn in Idaho could get," she said, rubbing her hands up and down her arms as if the friction would light some heat.

He gestured to the gate just beyond the rose arbor. "Come on, let's stop by the house and you can warm up."

She looked past the roseless vines to the tidy Tudor-style house. She'd only been in there twice as a kid. Dex's parents hadn't been crazy about her and it had always seemed easier to hang out at the hotel or the tree house.

Curiosity, cold and an admitted feeling of forbidden naughtiness to see what could happen when she and Dex were alone in a nonfreezing place stirred together in an explosive combination.

"I'd love to heat up," she told him.

Dex's smile was slow, intense and sexy. Zoe's body went into meltdown mode, despite her determination to watch her step. He pressed his hand into the small of her back, warming her as he guided her through the arched metal to his gate.

Typical of the small town, the front door was unlocked. "Can I get you something to drink?" Dex offered as he swung it open.

"Nah, I'm good."

She glanced over when he made a little choking noise in his throat. He met her eyes, his look pure innocent questioning.

"Through here," was all he said as he gestured.

Zoe looked around with unabashed nosiness as Dex led her from the tiled entryway to the large sunken living room. Muted colors, soft textures, simple lines. Much the way she remembered his parents. Not the kind to stand out, definitely on the quiet side.

"It's hard to picture you growing up here," she said as she peeked into the formal dining room while he stoked the fireplace embers into a nice flame.

Dex tossed her a questioning look over his shoulder, then glanced around the room. "Really? Why?"

"It's so mellow. You aren't really the mellow type."

Finished poking at the wood, Dex rose to his feet and crossed over to the large sectional couch. Apparently at ease with Zoe's nosing about, he dropped down and propped his arm over the back cushion.

"What type am I then?" he asked with an amused look that said he was humoring her joke.

She was serious though. Zoe considered him as she slowly walked over and dropped to the cushion next to him. She leaned one elbow on the back cushion and propped her chin on her fist.

"Driven," she said contemplatively. "Intelligent and so self-possessed that you often intimidated other people. You never seemed to care, though. You just did your own thing, regardless of what everyone else thought."

Dex pulled a face and shrugged. "Okay, I guess I did. But you did, too."

"No," she disagreed. "I might have done my own thing, but I never let go of worrying about what other people were thinking. Saying about me."

"But you never let that stop you. And you haven't changed, have you?" he said, his tone implying that she was to be admired.

"How do you figure?"

"You showed up at a reunion for a class you basically detested, wearing a leather dominatrix outfit and sporting a whip."

She smirked. "It was a crop."

"And I hear you wielded it well. Like I said, you have no problem rubbing their faces in your individuality," Dex mused. "You might wonder what they think, but you never let it keep you from following your own path."

Zoe smiled, pretending she agreed with his analysis. But she knew better. Worrying about what people thought of her was her standard MO. It had haunted her through high school, had molded her career and was dogging her now, even as she sat with the one person in the world she'd never had to worry about trusting.

"Did you ever find out who was behind the naked limbo contest?" she asked, changing the subject with a grin. She had to admit, the reunion games were turning out to be a lot less boring than they'd been in the agenda the committee had sent out.

Dex's sigh was a work of art. A hint of color washed his cheeks and he nodded his head ruefully.

"Who?" she demanded.

"My grandmother."

Zoe burst out laughing. "You're kidding!"

"She's also offering to help couples unblock their sexual chakra in the lobby, and she's matchmaking according to aura colors." He grinned and shrugged. "You might want to watch out for her."

"That'd account for the line waiting after she gave me that little reading," Zoe recalled with a giggle of delight.

"Probably."

"So what have you been doing with your life the past ten years?" she asked, changing the subject by leaning over to lightly punch him in the arm. Hey, any excuse to get a touch in.

"Nothing much," he dismissed, his beautiful eyes seeming to get a little distant. "I spent a few years at M.I.T., then went to work for a tech company. I specialized in strategic endeavors and applications. Made a lot of money, sent it home to help my parents, got burned out and here I am."

Zoe nodded. Definitely not creative. His explanation put to rest that tiny, nagging suspicion she'd had that he might, just maybe, be Gandalf. But people didn't go to M.I.T. for graphic design. And besides, she'd asked. He'd said no. And Dex wouldn't lie to her.

"I'll bet your parents really appreciated the help," she said instead. Even though the Drakes were one of the wealthiest families in town, Dex's dad had often lamented what a huge time—and money—pit the inn was. "I remember how stressed your dad always seemed to be trying to keep the inn going."

Dex gave a deprecating half smile and shrugged. "I suppose they appreciate it. They never really approved of me not taking over the inn, letting Dad retire, so to speak. But I toss enough financial help their way and they suck it up. I know the idea of me being out of work freaks them out."

"Maybe they're worried about you?" Zoe ventured.

When Dex snorted, she knew it was a waste of breath. He'd spent many an hour grumbling about his dad's expectations and how all he was to his parents was a future meal ticket. From the look on his face, that opinion hadn't budged over the years.

"If you're interested, I can make some calls," she offered hesitantly. Male egos were such a confusing, fragile thing. Even in crisis, they refused to admit they needed any kind of help. But she still had to offer. She wanted to do something for Dex. Even more, she wanted to build a new connection, a reason to keep in touch after this week was over.

Was it worth the risk of pissing him off, though? She thought of the empty months ahead if he slipped off her radar again and decided that, yes, for once, the risk was worth putting herself on the line.

"I've worked with a lot of companies, know tons of people. Maybe I can make some connections for you?" she continued tentatively. Those gorgeous eyes went round. Zoe held her breath, her tongue, and waited for the explosion.

DEX'S HEART WENT ALL soft and gooey, like a caramel brownie fresh from the oven. It was crazy to be so touched, but he was. Zoe didn't make offers like that as a rule, he knew. Not out of any lack of compassion. But she'd been mocked, turned down and pushed away so often as a kid, she'd pulled in to protect herself. She'd been different when she'd moved to town at fifteen, never in step with the other kids in Bradford. When talk about her mom and the high-school principal and how that played into her parents' marriage problems had become gossip fodder, she'd taken that protective layer and turned it into a wall. When they'd died, the wall became unbroachable.

That she'd peek over the wall and offer to help him said volumes. Even though he knew he shouldn't touch her, should be careful in case he gave away the fact that she had a damned good reason not to trust him, Dex gave in to the need.

He reached over and, a huge grin splitting his face, gave her a quick hug. That quick embrace was enough to remind his body of the glorious pleasure hers offered. He let go as though she was on fire. Nope, if he was going to keep his dick in his pants, he needed to keep his hands to himself, too.

"You're sweet," he said, forcing himself to focus on her gesture instead of the delicious curves his mouth watered to taste under her sweater. "But I'm fine. I have a few things in the works that should pan out, set me up for the next stage of the game. I can't really talk about them, though."

"Superstitious?" Zoe asked with a knowing nod.

"Sure." That worked as well as anything. "You save those connections, those favors, for your own climb up the ladder."

Zoe smirked. "Do you really think I go anywhere near the ladder?"

"Nah, not really. I'm surprised you're working for yourself, though. Don't you ever want a little of that famed job security I hear is so popular?"

"I like freelancing," she said with a shake of her head. The move sent her curls tumbling around her cheeks. Dex's fingers itched to wrap one of those ringlets around his finger. To use it to anchor her in place so he could brush his lips over hers. "I work for myself, set my own time frames, answer to nobody for long. It suits me."

So her words said. But her eyes were a different matter.

Dex wondered if she'd ever seen the worry in them. The faint lines of stress and questioning.

"I guess the jetting off to exotic locales, the excitement of meeting new people all the time, the challenge of starting from scratch with each job, is pretty hard to beat, huh?"

Zoe snorted, her eyes mocking his description.

"Podunk nowheresville, which is where I always seem to end up, isn't exactly exotic. I'm not a people person, but I've developed some awesome avoidance skills. But the starting-from-scratch part? That has definite appeal. I just go in, do the job without worrying about politics or pissing anyone off, then I'm on my merry way."

Dex had to grin, easily seeing the attraction that would have for Zoe. She never had been the ass-kissing, ladder-climbing type. But given her history, he'd think a little security would be a good thing.

"Don't you worry about the future?" he mused. "You know, job security, retirement, group health discounts?"

He waited for her blithe brush-off. Zoe? Worry about health insurance?

"A little," she said quietly, her gaze sliding away from his as though she was admitting an ugly secret. "Mostly I love working for myself. But sometimes I worry about the future."

"Have you ever thought about a…well…not a normal job," he said with a grin, "but something with a little wider safety net?"

She gave a jerky shrug and got up to wander the room, as if just talking about a real job made her itchy.

"I had an offer recently," she admitted quietly as she poked at the magazines his mom kept fanned out on the side table. "Great company, lots of wiggle room."

"But?"

"But it's a long-term commitment. They'd be counting on me, I'd be stuck with them. What if…" She trailed off, then shrugged. With a grin, she tugged one of the magazines out of the stack and held it up. "No big. How trippy is this? Since when is your mom a video-game buff?"

Dex stared blankly at the manga-ish cartooned magazine in her hand. What was that doing here? He squinted, noting it was the first to feature one of his games, the debut of SweetCheeks, so to speak. He hadn't realized his mom had bought the issue, let alone saved it. Pride, confusion and worry that Zoe would connect the dots urged him to jump out of his seat and grab it away from her.

Not too subtle, so he did the next best thing. He distracted her. "Better than skin magazines."

She laughed, then riffled through the rest of the stack. "Good point. No skin here." Then she shot him a naughty look. "Your grandma didn't say you were big on visual help when she detailed our sex life."

"I'm a very visual person," he assured her. Then, even knowing he was asking for trouble, he let his gaze wander over her body. Knowing what lay beneath her loose sweater and hiphugging jeans only added to the desire in his stare.

Her breath hitched, making her breasts shift intriguingly beneath the black fabric. His eyes narrowed, his dick stirred. She licked her lips and Dex gave an almost-silent groan.

Zoe tapped her fingers on her hip for a few seconds, then obviously making up her mind, she came back to the couch and sat. Only this time, she didn't leave any space between them. One knee curled under her, she leaned closer.

"What kind of visuals turn you on?" she asked, her tone husky, her eyes hesitant.

In those dark depths, Dex could see the risk that worried him, too. The fear of ruining a memory, of stepping over a line.

"I'm not big on mass seduction," he admitted. "Magazines, skin flicks, they don't mean anything."

"What about personal seduction?"

"When it's done right..."

"I'm always right," she teased. A tiny, wicked grin flirted with the corners of her mouth.

His own mouth watered to taste her again. His heart beat so loudly, it played a cacophony in his head. His dick swelled painfully.

He wanted her so badly. He had to taste her again.

With that in mind, he leaned close. Inches from her mouth, he saw her eyes lose that sleepy seductive look and go wide in horror.

"This is a bad idea," she said abruptly, pulling back. She looked as if she was controlling her urge to run from the room.

Hurt quickly followed by anger punched through Dex's belly. What? Was she only attracted to him if he wore a mask? Going with the anger, Dex wanted to pound on the couch in frustration.

"I don't…" She swallowed, closed her eyes and looked as though she was trying to find the words. Dex's anger turned down from boil to simmer as he watched her struggle.

"We're friends," she said, opening her eyes to meet his. A sweet sort of misery lurked in those green depths. "I don't call many people *friend,* Dex. And you're the best I've ever had. I don't want to risk that."

Friends. Dex was torn between howling like an angry wolf and beating his head against the fireplace bricks.

"Are you saying you're not attracted to me?" he asked baldly.

Her laugh was a gurgle of pained amusement. Zoe gave a rueful shake of her head and told him, "I'd be a liar if I said I didn't want to climb all over you and do wild things to your body."

Dex grinned and shifted toward her. She held up her hand.

"But we're friends."

Like that was poison to passion or something? Dex frowned, marshaling his arguments. Then he saw the look in her eyes—confusion twisted with lust. And there, beneath it, that little-girl-lost expression that had always torn at his heart when they'd been kids.

"Sure, we're friends," he said with a sigh. "But that doesn't mean it can't be more, Zoe."

"Dex, you're the sweetest guy I know. The absolute best." Zoe hesitated, then leaned forward and brushed a soft, feathery kiss over his cheek. With a bittersweet smile, she rose and headed for the door. "There's very little from my past that means more to me than our friendship. I don't want to ruin that."

Damn. There was nothing she could have said that would more effectively tie his hands.

There was nothing sweet about the way he wanted her. It took everything he had for Dex not to leap up off the couch, grab her, toss her to the floor and show her just how wild and dirty he could be.

"Why did you come to the reunion?" he asked. Frustration fueled the words, but he really wanted to know.

"It wasn't to ruin our friendship," she said defensively. Dex just raised a brow, not needing to point out the useless-ness of stating the obvious.

She shrugged, then reached for the doorknob. "I'm here to find some guy named Gandalf. If you have any tips, I'd appreciate them. Because as soon as I figure out who he is, I'll be able to get the hell out of Dodge."

Gandalf again. That she wanted his alter ego and not him really chafed. Stubbornly, Dex kept silent.

When he didn't say anything, she sighed and rolled her eyes. "Dexter, you'll thank me later. Sex would be mind-blowingly great, sure. But some things are more important than that. Don't you think so?"

He groaned. She smiled, obviously thinking he'd taken it as a joke. Except he could still recall the taste of her, the scent of her juices when she exploded beneath his tongue. Definitely not something he'd joke about.

"Look, I'll get out of your way. But if you come up with

any deets on that Gandalf guy, I'd appreciate it." He heard her mutter as she closed the door behind her, "I wouldn't mind knowing who the hell his friend Aragorn is, either."

Dex didn't know how long he sat there on the couch staring at the front door, the echo of Zoe's parting comment ricocheting around in his head. He watched her departure through the window, trying to grapple with this latest twist.

She wanted his alter ego for career purposes. She wanted his costumed self for sexual thrills. And the real him? He was regulated to the corner wearing a stupid "The woman I'm crazy about came to town and all I got was this stupid *friend*" stamp on his forehead.

To hell with that.

He was a smart man. He'd figure out a strategy to change Zoe's mind. But, like any smart man, he knew the benefit of narrowing the competition. To do that, he had to find out why she wanted Gandalf. Then he'd be able to strategize his game plan. Because there had never been a prize in Dex's life that was more important to win than Zoe.

With that in mind, he headed for his childhood bedroom. There, he booted up his laptop and flexed his fingers. First, some research into Zoe's consultation clients. Then he'd play. It had been a few years, but he was pretty sure his hacking skills were still top-notch. The hardest part, he knew, would be waiting around for her to log onto her own computer.

9

ZOE STEPPED OUT of the bathroom, steamy heat following her in a misty, fresh-scented cloud. It had taken twenty minutes under the hot shower to thaw out her toes.

Both to ask around and to promote Julie's quest to be queen, Zoe'd had lunch with the math club, then spent a few hours shopping in town with the yearbook committee. She probably should have stopped there, but she was desperate to keep her mind off Dex and the stunned look of frustration he'd worn when she'd walked out. So she'd gone on the afternoon social hike that the not-popular-enough-for-Candice's-radar gang had organized.

Despite her confusion and worry over Dex, she'd been totally shocked to find she actually enjoyed most of the people she'd talked with. Sure, some were stuffy, others still dorks. But at least half had been…well, fun.

She might even join their spa day tomorrow before the dinner announcing the nominations for reunion king and queen. Anything to keep her mind off Dex. Not that she was having much luck with that. Not with avoiding Dex, thinking about Dex or talking to other people who were so impressed with how freaking wonderful Dex was.

She growled low in her throat, tugged the towel off her hair and tossed it across the room. Eight hours had done nothing to dull the sharp misery of denying herself the sweetest taste of heaven she'd ever been offered. Her body screamed that she should have gone for it, had sex with Dex and let the chips fall where they may. It wasn't as if one wild bout of passion—or five or six—meant forever. Except Dex was at his family's inn taking care of long-term responsibilities, and he had a grandma who predicted his wedding and kids.

He was just too good for the likes of a leather-wearing gal like her. Sure, he might be a little upset now. But he'd be more upset if she'd let them get intimate then broken his heart.

Throwing her towel-clad self on the bed, Zoe yanked open the nightstand for her candy stash. Popping a chocolate-covered caramel-nut treat into her mouth, she tugged her laptop over and booted it up. Before the welcome screen flashed, her cell phone rang.

She glanced at the screen and sighed. Then, pressing speakerphone, she answered. "No, Meghan. I haven't found your guy yet."

"You make it sound like that's the only thing I ever call you about," her sister-in-law defended, her tone pure irritation.

Only this week. Zoe uncapped her lotion and shrugged, but didn't respond.

"I miss you," Meghan told her. "I wanted to see how you're doing."

"Sorry, I'm feeling a little raw," Zoe said with a sigh. "I'm coming to find out that most of these people are actually pretty cool. Which makes me a total jerk for figuring them all for jerks just because a few made my life hell, ya know?"

"You're making friends?"

"I wouldn't go that far," Zoe headed her off. At the word *friends,* the image of Dex's face when she'd rejected him flashed behind her eyes. She hated that she'd put that look in his beautiful eyes. "I don't think I'm friend material," she decided. "I'm too much of a flake."

"You're my friend."

"That's because you married my brother and forced yourself on me."

Meghan laughed, even though they both knew it was pretty much the truth. People were fluid in Zoe's life. Except Zach. And by association, Meghan.

"You're not a really a flake," Meghan defended musingly. "You need to give yourself a chance. I think you're harder on yourself than anyone else would ever be. But you're brilliant, Zoe. You need to give people a chance to find that out."

"Yeah, yeah," Zoe muttered.

"What about that cutie you saw your first day there? Was he in your class?"

"He turned out to be Dex."

"The old friend?"

"Yeah. The old *best* friend. Why do guys have to be so complicated and confusing?" Zoe asked in exasperation as she rubbed the forest-scented lotion into her skin.

"Oh, please, guys are easy. You just complicate things by trying to avoid letting people know you. You might try dating sometime," Meghan continued in her big-sister-lecturing tone, "instead of always avoiding people."

Zoe made a face at the phone. She didn't avoid people. She simply chose not to deal with them long-term. Which is why the masked hottie was perfect for her. Limited time together, sexy possibilities. No commitments. Wild sex, intense passion, mind-blowing orgasms. And a happy wave of the fingers when it was over.

And then there was Dex. He made her think commitment. Which scared the hell out of her. She was crazy about two guys and she wanted them both like crazy. She didn't know what to do about it. She'd never been promiscuous. But now all she could think of was sex. Always and often. With both Dex and the masked hottie. Two men, both turning her on equally. Hell, if one of them suggested a threesome, she'd probably have herself stripped naked before they even shook hands hello.

Needing a distraction, Zoe glanced at her laptop. She listened with half an ear as Meghan lectured her on all the wonderful traits that Zoe should give herself credit for. Frowning, she stared at her computer screen. There, in the middle of the purple swirling wallpaper covered in hearts and skulls was a new icon. A glittering, circular arrow filled half her screen. It said, "C'mon, you know you want to."

Who'd touched her laptop?

She automatically ran a virus scan, then pulled out her jump drive. She'd backed up that morning, hadn't she?

"You're a great person, Zoe. You just need to give yourself credit." Meghan paused while Zoe snickered, then in a huffier tone continued, "How many sisters would drop everything to run off and try to help their brother, I ask you? Not many. And it might not even help now. Zach went on that interview."

Zoe checked the scan results. Clean. She plugged in her jump drive. All backed up. Intrigued, she finally let herself click on the icon.

Holy shit.

The icon opened a virtual room. One dominated by a bed, filmy curtains hanging from the ceiling and satin pillows mounding against the headboard. On the huge bed were two cartoonish figures. Naked. Very, very naked.

Zoe's mouth dropped.

"Microsoft offered him a job. He said he might take it."

Zoe's eyes rounded and she gasped. Oh, God. That naked cartoon girl was *her*.

"I know, it's a shock," Meghan continued, her tone teary. "I hate that he's giving up like this. But he said it's what he wants to do."

Zoe grunted. She'd figured out that the arrow keys would move her naked cartoon around. Up, down, up, down. The naked cartoon man's face was hidden by a mask, but his grin was clear. Zoe figured out how to move around the room to change the view and noted that the avatar looked amazingly accurate. Except…the tattoo was missing.

"Wow," she breathed. Whoever had created this was a genius. Video-game seduction. Was it Gandalf? Given that she was here to track down a video-game master, that wasn't a speculative leap. But, she peered closer, no. Gandalf hadn't created this. Not only was it missing her trademark tattoo, but like any artist, Gandalf had a distinctive style. Stark, edgy and animated. These were…well, real. Like people. Zoe stared in awe. She noted the company logo on the bottom of the screen. Avigraph. No, not the same company Gandalf worked at. Obviously, her masked hottie had hacking skills and an account with some new social networking program. And what a program it was! She moved her avatar back, noting the muscled physique of the sexy guy in the shadows. Yummy. Her heart raced a little, her blood warming. Animated porn. If she turned on her speakers would she hear a bump and grind soundtrack?

"I told him you were looking for Gandalf. He said we're crazy, but he sounded sort of hopeful. So, don't give up, okay?" Meghan's voice, coming from somewhere in the background, paused. Then, "Zoe? Are you upset that I told him?"

Zoe blinked a couple of times. "Upset?"

The male cartoon moved. Her heart damn near jumped through her chest and Zoe almost screamed. She watched his animated hand reach out to curve over her cartoon breast, the thumb brushing the nipple enticingly. Heat curled low in her belly. She blew out a breath.

"Nope, not upset."

"Do you want to talk about it?"

"No. I just have to, you know, process it. I'll talk to you later." She didn't take her eyes off the screen and the magic that cartoon guy was playing on her body as she hit the off key on her phone.

Her masked lover had created this? She noted at the bottom of the screen the word *Avigraph*. Was it like that Web site Second Life? Maybe her masked lover had just created avatars of the two of them but hadn't created the program? Her mind raced, trying to figure out the answers. All she knew was this guy had obviously hacked her computer. But how? When? He'd have had to have access to her room, wouldn't he? To her laptop at least, to turn it on?

Speaking of turn-ons. Zoe's breath caught in her chest as the male avatar jackknifed up, his abs rippling in cartoon sexiness. His mouth latched on to her turgid nipple. Zoe's own, non-cartoon nipples peaked in aching hardness.

His hand traced her body from nipple to waist, then down to the curls between her legs. As though he was actually touching her body, warmth dampened her core. His mouth released her nipple. Zoe almost groaned in disappointment. He took her cyber hand and, after sucking her fingers into his mouth, trailed it down over her bereft breast, then down the same path his own hand had taken. He pressed her fingers to the valley between her animated legs.

Zoe narrowed her eyes, then, realizing what he was asking, she gasped. Her heart revved. Mesmerized, she followed his unspoken request. Shifting the laptop next to her on the bed, she slid down to lie on her side. Using the touch pad in concert with her movements, she made her avatar mimic her. She slipped her fingers into her mouth, wetting them, then traced the wet temptation around her aching nipple. She didn't know how to make her avatar pinch or flick the flesh, but didn't let that detail stop her from pleasuring herself.

The animated man shifted, sliding down her body. His fingers covered hers, pressing so she could see finger marks on her drawn breasts. Then he lifted her thighs, draping them over his shoulders. Zoe groaned. Her hand dropped to her own thighs, her finger tracing her swollen lips, then flicking the throbbing nub already damp with desire.

He buried his face between her legs. Zoe closed her eyes, letting the images of yesterday's delight with the masked hunk fill her mind: the sensation of his tongue over her skin. His fingers driving her wild, her own musky scent filled the air as she worked her flesh. Eyes still closed, she abandoned the touch pad to tweak her nipple in time with the fingers of her other hand moving in, out, swirling, then plunging again.

The image of Dex's face, his flirty little grin, filled her head. She imagined it was his mouth working her, his fingers moving in and out of her aching body, sending her higher and higher. His tongue slick and hot over her pulsing flesh.

Her back arched. She gave a keening cry and let herself ride the wave as she gripped the blankets to anchor herself to earth. Stars exploded behind her closed eyes, the orgasm taking on the heat of a supernova.

Finally, her breathing slowed. Her heart rate evened out and Zoe opened her eyes. There, hovering over the masked hunk's avatar was a word bubble.

"Was it good for you?"

She laughed and looked at her keyboard helplessly. How did one assure a cartoon that the cyber sex had rocked?

"Just type." The next word bubble instructed.

So she typed. "It was great for me. How about you?"

"Almost perfect."

"Almost?"

"It'd be better if you were really here."

Her thighs, still damp with her own juices, quivered. She brushed her index finger over her throbbing nub and groaned. Just the suggestion of a repeat performance in real life was almost enough to make her come again.

His word bubble appeared again. "Want to try it in real life?"

Oh, yes. Zoe wiped her fingers on the abandoned towel and typed in, "When?"

"Tomorrow night."

"Where?"

"A special room."

"Why special?"

"Because if we do this, you're going to agree to a couple of conditions."

"What conditions?"

"The room is dark or you wear a blindfold. In exchange for you promising not to violate my secret identity, I'll provide as many orgasms as you want."

Zoe couldn't help it. She burst out laughing.

"How long do we have?"

"Twelve hours."

"What if I said two dozen?"

"Twenty-four orgasms, in exchange for your promise."

She snickered. "Did you want me to sign a contract?"

"Your word is all I need."

Zoe hesitated. Then, because she had to ask, she typed, "Are you Gandalf?"

She stared, unwilling to blink as she waited for the reply. Her eyes started to water.

Finally, "No."

Zoe's shoulders slumped. Well…that solved the moral issues of having sex with a guy she was chasing for a job. But it didn't help her help Zach.

"Why?" asked his word bubble.

If the man was going to give her twenty-four orgasms, she supposed she could 'fess up to her mission.

"That's why I'm here at the reunion," she typed. "I need to find him."

"Why?"

Zoe frowned, then tugged the blanket over her naked body. Suddenly she felt as though she was being interrogated. And that her cyber lover had a lot more information than he was sharing.

"I have a business deal for him. Do you know who he is?"

Silence. Zoe puffed out a breath and wondered where she'd taken a wrong turn. Only five minutes ago she'd been floating on a glorious sexual cloud. Now she felt naked and off-center.

Had she blown it all? Starting to feel pissy, she wondered if she cared.

"Maybe we should just forget this," she typed, her fingers stabbing at the keys.

"I'll be at your room tomorrow evening at eight to escort you."

And just like that, he was gone. Not only the word bubbles, but his avatar. Zoe blinked, and with a frown, closed her laptop rather than look at her lonely naked cartoon self.

ZOE SAT ON THE rickety wood floor of the tree house, her arms wrapped around her knees as she contemplated her ugly boots.

When did life become all about compromise? If she wanted to help her brother, she had to trip her way down memory lane. To find peace of mind without freezing her ass off, she had to give up her gorgeous boots for ugly footwear. To have incredible sex, she had to practically sign an anonymity clause.

So much for bucking all the rules and doing things her way.

To top it all off, yesterday's conversation with Dex still whirled through her mind. Was Meghan right? Was she running before she gave Dex a chance?

A rustling in the weeds below warned her that she wasn't alone any longer.

Curious, she looked through the opening in the floor.

"Hey," she greeted reluctantly when she saw Dex's face peering up at her. Had her thoughts drawn him to her? Or just luck? She hated that her shoulders tensed at the sight of his gorgeous eyes. "Look, I'm claiming territorial dibs here."

"Terms?"

"No games." She welcomed his company, but she wasn't up for another round of flirtation yo-yo.

"Deal."

She heard him step onto the first of the board stairs leading up the tree and grinned when he swore. Yeah, that's the board that'd ripped her jeans.

"You come here often?" His head poked through the floor.

She gave a reluctant smile. "Are you going to ask me my sign next?"

"Scorpio." Using his impressive biceps, he raised himself the rest of the way into the tree house. Much more graceful than her gasping, huffing struggle to pull herself in, she had to admit.

"Why aren't you playing reunion games?" he asked, sitting across from her and leaning his back gingerly against the rotting wood wall. "I hear my grandma's organized rounds of spin the bottle in the conference room."

Zoe cracked a smile.

"Not up to it," she said with a shrug. "I needed some think time. I figured there had to be some residual mulling energy in the tree house, so I risked life and limb—to say nothing of my jeans—" she gestured to the rip in the knee of her pants "—to cop a little nostalgia time."

"What are you thinking about?" he asked.

It didn't seem appropriate to tell him it was sex, so she settled for sharing her other issue. "Whether I was a total jerk in school or if everyone here has changed."

"You were never a jerk," he said with a frown.

"I worried you'd think I was one yesterday," she said softly.

"Does this mean you've changed your mind?"

She reluctantly returned his smile, but shook her head.

"I don't want to risk our friendship, Dex. I know I blew it before. I was a jerk and let our friendship go. I don't want to lose touch again." Trying to lighten the moment, she winked and said, "Maybe that'd be easier if I pretended I don't think you're gorgeous. But I can't lie to you."

As she'd intended, he smiled. But she saw frustration and something else in his eyes. It almost looked like guilt.

"You weren't a jerk," he muttered again.

Zoe shrugged. She had been. She'd shown up here with a huge chip on her shoulder and an attitude bigger than the state of Idaho. "I guess I thought, somewhere in the back of my head, that to do my job, to travel and be free to come and go, I had to do it unencumbered."

"You really do love your job," he noted.

"I do. And I've come to realize that I can love it and still have people in my life. Weird thing to come to a reunion that I thought I'd hate and find myself making new friends. I'm kind of excited about it."

He grinned. "You should always do what gets you excited."

She peered at his face, wondering if he'd meant the double entendre. But he looked as innocent as a baby. She gave a wicked grin. Which meant he probably did.

"Excitement is crucial," she agreed before she remembered her no-flirtation-games rule. She dropped her smile and shrugged.

"So is that your big goal this week?" he asked. "To collect as many friends as you can?"

"That's not what I intended," she admitted. "But it's turning into a nice unexpected benefit."

"Sometimes intentions get twisted up when we're faced with temptation." He hesitated, an intense look of contemplation on his face. Then he said, "Look, I need to tell you something."

She raised a brow. But before he could expand on that confession, his phone buzzed.

He pulled it out of the pocket of his black leather jacket, glanced at the screen and grimaced. "I need to get back. The morning manager is an idiot and apparently can't handle the linen delivery without someone to hold his hand."

"Your parents must be loving you for giving them this

break," she said, wondering how they stood the constant demands on their time. She could see how much it was stressing Dex out.

"They called this morning. I've never heard my dad sound so relaxed." Dex gave her a sheepish look. "He thanked me. I didn't realize my parents hadn't had a vacation in twelve years. Not since Gramps died. I guess it's no wonder Dad stresses about money all the time. This place is obviously getting to be a total pain in his ass."

He excused himself to deal with the text message.

Zoe's gaze fixed on the phone. She blinked. Her heart froze. It couldn't be. Zoe's mind raced. Confusion fought with emotions, her tangled thoughts in shock. Forcing herself not to gasp, she raised her eyes to search his face. He wasn't looking at her, luckily. Instead, she watched his beautiful eyes scan the message, then text something back.

"I've got to go," he said after a few seconds. Obviously unaware that her brain had gone numb, he hesitated, then leaned forward and brushed a soft, sweet kiss over the flesh visible through the tear in her jeans. "Sorry to kiss and run."

Zoe choked back a laugh. Ironic, given she was pretty sure now that this wasn't the first kiss-and-run he'd done to her. Although at least her pants were still on this time.

"Want to do dinner?" he asked.

Zoe didn't know what to say. Did she confront him? Ignore her discovery? Scream at him for hiding behind a mask?

She looked into his beautiful aquamarine eyes and for the first time, saw the struggle there. The risk he thought he was taking. Finally she understood why.

What she didn't understand was the reason behind the why.

Still numb, she wondered if she'd be angry when this all

settled into her brain. She watched the anxiety in his eyes, the worried crease of his forehead.

No anger. Only confusion. And the deep, heartfelt need to spend more time with him.

"Sure. Dinner's good." Then, unable to help herself, she taunted, "But it has to be early. I have an…appointment later."

Yeah. There it was. Just the flicker of his lashes. Probably undetectable by most people, but Zoe knew him. He was hiding something. And she was pretty sure she knew what.

But he only grinned, then traced a finger over her cheek before he dropped through the hole in the floor and out of sight.

She shook off the shock and checked through the window to make sure he'd gotten down safely.

Zoe watched Dex's fine ass as he hurried up the dry golden field of grassy dirt. Her mind raced in a million directions at once. But one thought stood out, crystal-clear.

Well, well. Zoe puffed out a breath and tried to corral her galloping thoughts.

She didn't know how or why. She didn't have a clue how she felt about it. All she knew was her geeky old friend Dex was the masked hunk, aka the most mind-blowing orgasm of her life.

The question was, what did she do about it? Cancel their rendezvous? Wasn't that like locking the barn door after the stallion had mounted the mare? Any risk to their friendship was already made.

Was she going to deny herself the best sex of her life on a futile principle? Or was she going to do what any smart, red-blooded woman in her position would do? Celebrate the fact that the two guys who made her crazy with lust were one and the same?

Looked like she was getting her three-way after all.

10

DEX PACED IN FRONT of the elevator, his hands shoved in his pockets. His brain raced, arguing with itself. He'd told Zoe he wasn't Gandalf. For all intents and purposes, that was true. He'd given up his pseudonym, right? So why was he itchy with guilt? He didn't owe it to her to tell her that he had been. Or was that just his ego talking, trying to keep her from speculating about Brad the dick again?

He ran a hand through his hair and wondered how he'd played himself into this corner. Only a month off the job and he'd already lost his ability to strategize and reason. That didn't bode well for running his own company. Then again, he wasn't competing with the likes of Zoe Gaston and her inimitable sex appeal in business, so maybe he'd be okay?

"Hey there, Dexter."

Dex turned with a frown, his shoulders tensing.

"Hello," he greeted the redhead cautiously. He was honestly surprised she knew his name. Of course, the last time she'd caught him alone in the hall, she'd plastered both hands over his ass and offered to show him heaven. But he had the impression that hadn't been anything personal.

"Are you going to see Zoe soon?" she asked with a friendly smile that had no hint of ass-grabbing threat.

"We're going to the reunion dinner together," he admitted

carefully. Just to be safe, he shifted so his hiney was as far from her hands as possible, too.

"Good." She glanced around, then stepped closer. Dex stepped back. Her eyes widened before they crinkled in amusement. "Your butt's safe with me. Watch out for my sister, though."

He narrowed his eyes. "Twins, right?"

A little of the tension in Dex's shoulders released when she nodded. He had enough to worry about with Zoe already, having her show up for their first date—unofficial though it might be—to find some other woman's hands on his ass was bound to set the evening back a bit.

"Can you pass on a message for me?" the redhead said quietly, her smile dropping away. "I overheard some of the guys talking about a bet. She's front and center and needs to watch out."

Dex frowned. He didn't know why her warning bothered him. No, he didn't want anyone hurting Zoe. But it was his job to watch out for her. Especially from members of the popular—aka, nasty—crowd. Like the redhead in front of him.

He saw a hint of honest worry in her eyes. Still, he didn't trust her. "Since when do you worry about Zoe's feelings?"

The friendly blue eyes turned icy. "Since I grew up. Something you apparently haven't experienced."

Dex frowned. He'd never experienced anything but friendliness—granted in an only-as-long-as-he-was-useful kind of way—from anyone in school, either.

"I'll watch out for Zoe," he vowed.

The redhead, Julie according to her necklace, gave a little sigh. Her eyes melted and she raised an amused brow. "Still crushing hard, hmm?"

Dex started to deny it. The Zoe stepped off the elevator.
His heart did its usual happy dance at the sight of her. So
did his dick when the full impact of her appearance hit him.
She was dressed for the night, as in, her dress looked like
a tiny little nighty. Short, strappy and sexy as hell. The
black silky fabric shot with shimmer draped lovingly over
her curves.

"Yep, crushing for sure," Julie answered her own question.

Dex ignored the redhead. He thought he murmured his
excuses as he walked away but he wasn't sure. All he knew was
Zoe was here and, thanks be to heaven, she was his for the night.

"Ready?" he asked as he reached her, only having to shove
two guys aside on the way over.

"Are you sure you want to go to this stupid reunion
dinner?" she asked, one hand smoothing over the lapel of the
sport jacket he'd thrown on over his T-shirt. "Maybe instead
you'd like to find somewhere private and share a few secrets?"

Secrets? Pulse racing, Dex scanned her face. Did she know?
There was no suspicion in her eyes, just amusement. Still, his
mind raced to the lie he was telling by going through with their
rendezvous. He had to tell her. He should tell her now.

But he couldn't. He had a chance at his dream night. Well,
not exactly a dream since his fantasies usually revolved
around Zoe calling his name during well-lit kinky sex. But this
was as close to his fantasy as he might ever get. Zoe wanted
her mystery guy. Not her geeky old friend. Between that and
her probable fury if she found out he'd deceived her, he was
sure telling her the truth was a one-way ticket to the end.

So he contented himself by smoothing his palm over her
shoulder and down her back. Her skin was warmer, silkier,
than the fabric of her tiny dress.

Later tonight, he'd get to run his tongue over that skin. Every delicious inch of it.

Holding tight to that thought, he gave Zoe an easy smile and shook his head.

"Well, it's not like I'd attend my own reunion. Might as well do yours and see what it's like," he said as he led her into the ballroom.

An hour later, he wished he'd taken her up on the invitation to skip out. "Is all the reunion stuff this boring?" he murmured in her ear as he pulled out her chair for dinner.

"Oh, yeah," she said with a wicked grin as she slid gracefully into the seat and shot him a naughty look over her shoulder. "Kissing ass, lying and barely veiled insults are only the highlights. Wait until they start the speeches about the good old days."

Before he could grab her hand and pull her out of the room, others joined their table. Trapped by the manners his mother had nagged into him, Dex sank into his chair with a grimace.

Resigned to polite small talk, he made Zoe laugh and kept her at ease as their table filled up and dinner was served. All the while, he fantasized about how she'd look later, when he could strip her out of that dress. Imagination was key, he knew, since he'd set the room up to be totally dark, with only a ten-watt bulb in the bathroom for safety.

Considering whether he could talk Zoe into blindfolded sex, he decided to toss a couple of candles into his bag.

Then he almost choked on his bite of chicken. A foot slid up his calf. A teasing, tempting, bare female foot. He glanced at the guy sitting to his left and refused to consider it might be his.

His gaze flew to Zoe's.

"Hungry?" she asked, her eyes innocent, her tone bland.

"Starving," he admitted. And just a little confused. Was Zoe playing footsie with him? And didn't she have a date later with…him?

"You should eat," she said huskily, leaning toward him so her dress gaped in a way that made his brain go numb. "You need your energy. Who knows what kind of craziness you'll have to deal with later."

"Later?"

"Yes, later." She trailed her fingers, just the tips, over the back of his hand. "You've been putting out one fire after another, remember? Your sweet granny might organize a panty raid or something."

"Right, that kind of craziness." Dex's brain told him her comment had been innocent. His instincts told him she was playing with him. Before he could call her on it there was a loud squeal as someone turned on the microphone.

"And our first nominee for reunion queen is…" the reunion chair called out over the still-chatter-filled room "…Zoe Gaston."

"What?" Zoe yelped, turning so fast she yanked the tablecloth with her and almost pulled it to the floor. The room exploded in a cacophony of whispers. Faces turned, people gestured.

"They just announced you're in the running as reunion queen," Dex realized, a huge grin splitting his cheeks. He turned to give Zoe a hug and realized she was pure white. "What's wrong?"

"I can't believe anyone actually…" She stopped and frowned, then shrugged. "I'm sure it's just to get back at Candice after she publicly announced I didn't have a chance. It's not me people nominated, just the anti-cheerleader."

Dex couldn't tell if she was excited or not. She looked more confused than anything. He wanted to grab her into his arms and protect her, which was probably crazy considering this wasn't *Carrie.*

"They could have nominated anyone if they wanted to do that," he pointed out. They both glanced at the stage as the redhead, Julie Fenton, and Candice Love, were called as the other nominees. The crowd gave each perfunctory applause, except for the football table, which went nuts at Candice's name. Unlike Zoe or Julie, the blonde got up and gave a speech. At the end of Candice's little cheer, Brad stood and did his football victory dance on the chair. He stared right at Dex while he did it, too.

"You can totally win this thing," Dex said with determination, turning back to Zoe.

"Win it? You're kidding, right? The whole thing is a joke. I didn't toss my name in the hat and I sure as hell don't want to win."

Dex frowned at the fury in her voice. He looked around the room and noted all the snarky looks being shot Zoe's way. He noted even more downcast eyes and shamefaced avoidance of his gaze. His eyes met Julie's as she stepped off the stage. Instead of looking thrilled with her nomination, she was giving Zoe a concerned glance.

"Why not win?" he asked, his attention split between Zoe, the room and his spinning thoughts trying to put it all together. "You're just as eligible, better-looking and definitely more worthy than anyone else here."

Zoe gave him an indulgent-friend eye roll, then shook her head. "It's not about me being a winner. This is on the same plane as them nominating me as the Virgin Queen. It's a joke."

As he always did when her virgin moniker was mentioned, Dex growled low in his throat. He should have kicked Brad

Young's ass back in high school for that and that alone. What kind of wimp was he that he'd let something that hurt Zoe so much go without retribution?

"I want to leave," she said, her expression closed. She'd pulled the walls in again, he realized. Without waiting, she tossed her napkin on the table, and shoe-clad once more, she got up and rushed from the room.

Ignoring Brad's taunting call and Julie's worried look, Dex hurried after her. He caught her in the lobby and pulled her into one of the small private coves off to the side.

"Hold up," he said. "You don't know it's a joke. Maybe some people think you're worthy of being queen."

"Right," she agreed with more than a hint of sarcasm.

"You know, you don't always have to expect the worst," he admonished, a little pissed that she was so quick to doubt herself. "Haven't you met anyone since you've been here who wasn't a jerk?"

He saw the denial in her eyes, then the look shifted to contemplation. Then, as Zoe always did when she didn't want to deal with things, he watched her shove the whole issue aside.

Glancing around as if she'd just noticed where they were, a slow, wicked look crossed Zoe's face. To one side was a naked replica of the Venus de Milo, to the right was a huge potted plant. Pseudo privacy.

"Is this where you bring all your dates to say goodnight?" she said, putting an obvious effort into her teasing tone.

"Is the evening over?"

She took his wrist and turned it so she could see his watch. He noted it was about forty minutes from the time she'd agreed to meet the masked man.

"I do have some things to do," she said softly, her eyes now inspecting his face as if she could uncover all his secrets. Dex's spine stiffened at the thought.

Then she gave him a long, slumberous look that made his insides turn to molten lava. He stepped back.

She stepped closer, so close her scent wrapped around him like a lover's fingers. Dex gulped. A dull roar filled his head. It took him a second to realize it wasn't his racing heart, but the reunion dinner getting out. People filled the lobby behind them, reminding him that their privacy was a joke.

Whoa, dude, he told himself. He'd get a taste later. He just had to stick to the plan. Zoe took another step forward, ignoring the hoots and hollers of the football jerks passing behind them.

Apparently Zoe wasn't on board with the plan. Nor did she seem to care they had an audience.

"I hate to ruin a great evening by asking a stupid question," he said, picking his words like steps through a live minefield, "but what are you doing?"

"Wasn't this evening a date?" she asked in a husky tone.

Dex swallowed. His hands automatically found her hips through the silken fabric of her dress. The material slid over her skin in an erotic temptation, reminding him of what he'd tasted the day before. Of what he hoped to taste again tonight.

If he didn't blow it.

"I don't know that I'd define it as a date, exactly," he hedged, the little voice in the back of his head asking what the hell harm one little kiss could do. It wasn't as if he could only kiss one way, right? It wouldn't be a total giveaway, would it? "It was more like two good friends. Two old friends, getting together for dinner and, you know, a good time."

Zoe wrapped her arms around his neck, her fingers tangling in his hair. He almost moaned aloud as they wove sensuously through the strands. He reached up to pull them down, but only managed to wrap his fingers around her wrists before his willpower deserted him.

HER MOUTH INCHES FROM paradise, Zoe ignored the hoots and catcalls behind them. She wanted to wipe the doubts and fears from her mind, and kissing Dex was the perfect way to do it. Irritation filled her belly. Leave it to those jerks to find her secluded corner and ruin the rest of her evening with Dex. She could have tried to drag him off somewhere more private, but she didn't have a lot of time. She had to hurry if she wanted to get back to her room with time for a quick do-me prep before her hot date. She gave a mental laugh when she realized her hot date was with Dex, too.

"I like to finish my good times with a good-time kiss," she said, trying to make the words soft and seductive. If the dilation of Dex's eyes was any indicator, she'd succeeded. Zoe closed the distance between their bodies. She didn't press herself against him, just…hovered. Every breath he took brought his chest against her silk-covered breasts.

She didn't take his suddenly sucking in and holding his breath as an insult. She took it as a triumph. Especially when he gave her a helpless look and dropped his hands from her wrists.

"Zoe, this is crazy."

"I'm not asking you to strip naked and let me ride you in the lobby," she chided. "Just a simple, goodnight kiss."

After all, that was all she'd need to prove to herself that the guy she'd felt up with her foot tonight was the same one who'd had her as his yummy snack two days before. And, in a twisted way, she would extract a little bit of revenge.

"After one kiss, you might be the one stripping," he warned, his hands once more settling on her hips.

Zoe grinned. "You wish."

"Absolutely," he murmured as he gave in to the temptation and lowered his mouth to hers.

Zoe had memorized the kisses of the past few days. She could close her eyes and replay the intense power of the masked hunk's tongue as it demanded entry into the wet heat of her mouth. She knew intimately how he would swirl his tongue, use it to send shafts of electric desire shooting through her system.

This kiss wasn't the same. This kiss coaxed rather than demanded. His lips brushed a soft seduction over her lips, gentle and sweet. She parted her own in a deep, romantic sigh. He used the opportunity to slide his tongue between her teeth, teasing and tempting hers to play. Her knees went weak. Heat, sweet and syrupy, dampened her panties.

No. Not the same, but so deliciously sensual.

Dex pulled away slowly. Zoe gave a little hum of pleasure and let her eyes flutter open.

"I've got to go," he said, stepping back as though she were a flaming effigy.

He turned away. Took two steps. Turned back to face her, then shrugged and shook his head. Then he took off.

Zoe held back her laugh until he was out of hearing distance. Humming a satisfied tune, she sauntered toward the elevator to her room. That'd gone well. She grinned to herself and gave a little sensual shiver of delight. The stunned, slightly terrified look on Dex's face had more than made up for his hiding his identity from her.

Stepping into the elevator, she tried to reconcile this kiss and the masked hunk. The techniques were definitely different. The masked hunk was all about the thrust and parry. Hot, dangerous, sexual demand. Dex's kiss had been sweet seduction. Soft, gentle, but with an undercurrent of sensual wildness that would be a pleasure to coax into action.

But no matter how he tried to disguise it, she knew both sets of seductive lips belonged to Dex.

She knew she should be pissed at him. She'd even tried to be, for a whole ten minutes after she'd realized he was her masked hunk.

Then she'd remembered the struggle in his beautiful eyes. The worried frown and hesitance whenever they'd gotten close. If he really was her masked lover, whatever his reasons for hiding, she was sure he wasn't trying to screw her over. Not Dex. He was the only person other than her brother who she totally trusted.

So instead of giving him grief, she'd teased him a little. God, it'd felt good, too. Leave it to Dex to come up with an alternative makeout technique to keep her wondering about his identity.

Which sounded so calculated.

Zoe sighed and told herself to simply trust for once. Trust her instincts. Trust her own needs and desires.

She used her card key to let herself into her room.

And if she was a little biased in her argument, well, so be it. After all, she was about to spend the next twelve hours having the best sex of her life.

BLINDFOLDED, Zoe held a warm male hand and let its owner lead her down a narrow hall. She hoped like hell it was a deserted hall, although pictures of her with a bandana over her eyes would probably nix that stupid queen nomination. Her other senses amplified by the lack of sight, she heard steps against the carpet, hers and her seducer's, then the click of a lock as he opened a door.

Her pulse quickened, whether from nerves or anticipation she wasn't sure. What a way to start a sexual extravaganza. With a blindfold over her eyes and a duffel bag full of black leather over her shoulder.

"You brought the costume?" The masked hunk's voice verified as he led her into the room. Even through the bandana, Zoe could tell the room was pitch-black. How could he see? Then she noted a faint beam of light from one corner as she turned in a circle.

"Costume and crop," she verified. "But I have to tell you, I'm not sure I'm big on spankings."

"I might be," he teased.

It was that tone, the light laughter shimmering under his words that finally clinched it for her. Yes, the masked hunk was her Dex. The last knot of tension in her stomach dropped away. She'd deal with his reasons later. For now, it was enough to know who she was going to have wild, crazy sex with.

Tiny tendrils of tension Zoe hadn't even realized she was holding on to drained from her shoulders at the realization. Safe. As hot as anonymous, blindfolded sex probably was, just knowing that she'd be doing it with someone she trusted made it so much easier. So much better. The butterflies in her stomach shifted from nervously flapping their wings to doing a soft, excited dance of anticipation.

"Do I get to spank you?" she teased in return.

"Only if I don't completely satisfy you."

No spankings on the agenda, then.

"What first?" she asked. She realized she was talking to

make noise. Not being able to see added a wickedly exiting dimension to this little encounter.

She sensed his hand, felt the heat from his body before he reached for her. Zoe's entire body tingled as he slid the bag off her shoulder. She heard the muffled thump as it hit something. A chair, she thought. Good call; why clutter up the bed when their bodies were going to need it to roll around on.

The air moved between them as he shifted again, bringing his body in alignment with hers. Trusting her instincts, Zoe reached out, pressing her palm against the hard planes of his chest. His heart beat, steady and strong, beneath her fingertips.

She reached out with her other hand, tracing blindly up the side of his throat, over the sculpted planes of his jaw until she found his mouth. She ran her index finger over the fullness of his lower lip. She felt his heart pick up under her palm as she slid her finger into his mouth. He sucked, then gently bit down. Zoe's breath caught. Wet heat spun from her finger down to her core, making her squirm.

He curled his hand over hers, flattening her fingers so he could press a wet kiss to the center of her palm. At the same time, his hand pressed between her legs, mimicking the pressure of his heated kiss. Zoe gasped, her fingers curling over his pec, kneading like a pleasured cat.

He let go of her hand. She dropped it to his chest with the other, sliding both down the hard planes of his body, over the washboard stomach she couldn't wait to press her cheek to and down to tug his shirt from his pants. She buried her hand under the soft fabric, against the warmth of his skin. Used her fingers to trace along the waistband of his jeans, skimming them between the fabric and his warm belly.

Totally tuned in to his body, she could feel the pressure his
hard-on was putting on the fabric, tightening it against her
fingers. Zoe dipped one hand deeper, using the tip of her nail
to scrap the head of his straining dick through the soft cotton
of his boxers.

His groan filled her ears like a symphony, bringing both
joy and deep emotional satisfaction. Yeah, he'd promised her
a couple of dozen orgasms, but she'd like to give him just as
many. Not to win the game, but because she wanted him to
feel as good as possible.

As good as he made her feel. That deep-seated desire to
put his needs first hit her in a wave. Zoe's heart tumbled. Not
a sexual reaction, although there was plenty of that swirling
through her body, but for the first time in her life, in emotional
connection.

Impatient now, she pulled her hands from his pants and,
feeling her way to her objective, tugged at his belt. Before she
could figure out which way was which, Dex's hand covered hers.

"Wait," he commanded.

"Now," she demanded.

"Naked."

Zoe let go of his leather belt and reached for the buttons
on the front of the babydoll-style dress she'd changed into
after her shower.

"Let me," he said, his hands stilling her fingers again. His
hands on her waist, he guided her backward. The back of her
thighs hit the higher-than-normal mattress. Obeying his
unspoken command, Zoe sat.

She ran her tongue over her lips, her mouth suddenly dry
with nerves. It didn't feel like an easy game anymore. Oh, she
still felt like she was going to win. But the stakes had just been

raised. Her heart told her they might be out of her reach, tha
winning might cost her more than she'd been willing to bet

The backs of his fingers brushed the sides of her breast
as he unbuttoned her dress. Zoe waited for a caress, but non
came. When he reached the last button, he gently pushed th
silky fabric off her shoulders. She sucked in her stomach. Wh
was it so much more intimidating having someone look at yo
half-naked when you couldn't see their expression, she won
dered. Zoe heard his intake of breath.

A soft gust of air preceded his mouth as he pressed a tin
trail of kisses over the tops of her breasts, featured to the
fullest in her favorite lacy black push-up bra.

Her nipples puckered against the suddenly scratchy lace
need making them ache. He unsnapped the front hook with
tiny snick, unwrapping her swelling mounds in gentle, almos
reverent moves.

She arched her back. Dex ignored her silent plea, though
Instead, he cupped his hands under her hips, urging her bac
to her feet. Zoe stood, her legs still against the bed. She fe
it give and realized he'd climbed onto the mattress behind he

His fingers tangled in her hair, gathering it at her nape an
moving it aside.

She felt his breath first.

The moist heat made her shiver, despite its warmth. Zoe'
heart skipped double time as his other hand trailed, ever s
softly, down her arm. As his fingers trailed over the back o
her hand, then up the sensitive skin of her inner arm, h
brushed gentle, teasing kisses over her nape and down he
spine between her shoulder blades. He curled both hand
around the sides of her waist, then slid them up to cup he
breasts. His fingers traced a delicate, torturous design aroun

her nipples. No pressure, just a soft wispy sort of teasing that made her want to scream.

Zoe locked her knees to keep her legs from sagging.

He shifted, his hands sliding down her sides in a gentle dance as his mouth trailed down her spine. His lips reached the small of her back at the same time his palms arched around her pelvic bones. The tips of his fingers brushed the curls sheltering her damp, aching center.

Blindfolded, Zoe's senses were all attuned to his fingers, to the warmth of his mouth as he kissed the sensitive curve of her back. She could feel his breath, the sweet pressure of his fingers as they slowly slid through the silky curls between her legs. Zoe mewled a tiny cry of pleasure as his fingers pressed against the wet, swollen bud between her thighs.

Before she could do more than shudder with pleasure, though, he shifted. Startled, she gasped as his hands swung her around, the movement putting her off balance without sight. Her back landed on the mattress with a soft bump, her thighs automatically spreading to welcome his weight as he kneed between them.

Instead of a gentle teasing, his fingers tweaked and tormented her turgid nipples. Zoe sank her own fingers into his thick hair, using the soft strands to guide his head up to hers. Feeling his breath on her face, she lifted her head and instinctively found his mouth with her own.

Their tongues tangled in a wild dance. His hands left her breasts. From the sound of rustling fabric, the soft thuds against the carpeted floor, Zoe knew he was stripping. She released his hair to let her own hands explore the delicious hardness of his chest. She smoothed her hands even lower and with a little growl of appreciation, discovered he'd shucked his pants, as well.

Before she could avail herself of the naked treat her fingers were reaching for, he shifted. She held her breath, waiting to feel where he'd go, what he'd do next. His mouth joined his hands on her breasts, tongue swirling, then nipping. Zoe arched her back, pleasure exploding through her body like a power surge.

She shifted her hips upward, her thighs brushing against his thick, muscular legs. Arousal twisted in her belly, tightening her wet folds in need. She wrapped her legs around his waist, urging him closer, undulating against his body in supplication.

His hands cupped her breasts, pressing them closer together; his teeth scraped over her nipples. One, then the other, then back. He was driving her crazy.

Her breath coming in short gasps, Zoe's fingers gripped his biceps, the feel of the strong, hard muscles turning her on as much as his talented lips did.

"I need…" Her words were drowned out by his mouth as it took hers. As if reading her mind, he moved. The bed shifted by her shoulder as he planted one hand there for balance. With her feet anchored to the small of his back, she felt him rear back. There was a rustle of foil. Condom? The complete darkness added a sensual surrealism, making her feel like this was all one incredible wet dream.

The mattress shifted by her other shoulder. She felt his body tense beneath her hands, her calves, then he took her. One swift, forceful plunge and Zoe saw stars against the black blindfold.

She met each thrust with a roll of her hips, her inner walls gripping the thick length of him as he took her in a wild dance of pleasure.

For the first time in her life, Zoe was engulfed in sensations. Whether it was the kinky aspect of the blindfold or the trust it mandated, she couldn't hold anything back. Her entire being gave itself over to the intense power of sexual delight.

Dex's face flashed in her mind, filling her imagination. The visual of his aquamarine eyes, his quirky smile was all it took to send her over the edge.

Gasping little cries of satisfaction sang out as her body stiffened. Tight and needy, she flew into the darkness, her body shuddering in ecstasy.

As if he'd been waiting for her, Zoe's felt her cries spark his own orgasm. She felt him throb inside her, his body going rigid. One more thrust, then two and he growled low in his chest as he exploded. The sound, the feel of his climax sent Zoe over the edge again.

She mewled, tiny little waves of ecstasy washing over her, carrying her from intense fulfillment to gentle, sweet contentment. Slowly, as though she were floating off a cloud, Zoe landed. With a happy sigh, she cuddled closer to the man who'd just introduced her to heaven.

"That's two," he murmured against her hair as he gathered her tight in his arms.

11

DEX AWOKE WITH A start. It took him two seconds to orient himself. He'd removed the clocks from the room earlier, but he didn't think he'd slept long. Maybe fifteen, thirty minutes at the most. Even so, he was irritated. He didn't want to waste a single second, let alone a half hour of his time with Zoe. He had a plan for tonight. Wow her with the best sex of her life, then, when she was too exhausted from satisfaction to swipe at him, tell her the truth about his identity.

For a second he stared into the blackness of the room and wondered if this was just another dream. He'd had so many about Zoe over the years. But he could feel her breath against his shoulder, her heart beating gently against his chest. The silky fabric of the blindfold he'd tugged off her when they'd curled up together lay under his shoulder.

And, he realized as he flexed his leg, he had a cramp in his calf from trying to keep them angled away from the faint light shining under the bathroom door.

"Mmm."

Zoe's murmur of satisfaction did more to assure him it was all real than any of the rest. Dex grinned, letting his head fall back on the pillow as he did a silent whoop of joy.

"More?" he murmured, his hand sliding down her back to curve over the sweet roundness of her hip.

"Definitely," she said quietly. She suddenly gave his chest a push. Surprised, Dex fell sideways. Taking advantage of his shift, she squirmed out from under him and with amazing dexterity for a woman moving in a pitch-black room, straddled his hips.

She slapped her hands to his chest and, pressing him against the mattress, gave a little wiggle. Dex grinned in the dark as her seductive movements awakened his half-sleeping libido.

"This time, I'm in charge," she told him as she scraped her nails gently down his chest. Dex's breath caught when she skimmed them back up and flicked his nipples. He grabbed her hips, moving her down a few inches so her damp curls rubbed over his hardening dick.

Zoe purred, then shifted and let her hands fall on either side of his head. Dex felt the mattress compress just before her mouth found his. Tongues slid in a sinful dance, twisting sinuously. Zoe called the shots. Her mouth drove him crazy while at the same time she started an undulating move, swirling her hips in a clockwise torment over his straining dick and her breasts in counterclockwise bliss over his chest.

Dex groaned into her mouth. Taking that as a signal, Zoe pulled away, using her body to stroke his as she moved downward. Dex's breath stuck somewhere between his chest and his throat as she headed straight south.

Her stiff nipples marked a burning trail down his belly and over his thighs.

In typical Zoe fashion, she didn't play around but got right to the point of the game. Her fingers wrapped around the base of his dick, skating up and down in such a natural, seductive way that Dex felt as if she was reading his mind. Or had watched him pleasure himself and knew exactly how he liked it. The idea sent another surge of desire straight down between his legs. She moaned her approval as his dick grew proportionally.

Teasing, tempting, she ran the tip of her tongue over his straining head. Dex groaned.

Then she took him in her mouth and sucked. Playing his body like it was an instrument and she was a virtuoso, Zoe used her tongue and lips to send him straight into orbit.

Her mouth worked its sweet seduction, sliding up and down, sucking hard while he gripped the blanket in an attempt to keep from exploding. Heaven. Her mouth was the most amazing thing in the world. Dex panted, almost relieved when she pulled back to trace her tongue, just the end of it, over his wet, throbbing head.

Then she sucked. Just the tip of his dick. He gasped. The world spun once, then twice. Then Dex grabbed for the infinitesimal thread of control still in his reach. Releasing the blanket, he pressed both hands to her shoulders.

"Stop," he begged.

"Come," she challenged, her breath teasing his aching head.

Dex laughed. Even now, her mouth hovering at the throbbing tip of his dick, and she could make him laugh. Was it any wonder he loved this woman?

"I will," he promised. "But I want to come inside you."

His hands gripped her shoulders, pulling her up toward him. She resisted at first, then with a wet kiss to his already straining hard-on, she followed his unspoken request and rose. Torturing him, she nibbled her way up his body.

"Spoilsport," she muttered as she curled against his chest for a hug.

"Hey, you're the one with the mandate for twenty-four orgasms," he said as he finished reciting the state capitals and getting control of his libido. "You put me out of commission this early in the game and we might fall a few short."

Zoe giggled. He felt her shake her head, her hair a silky blanket ruffling over his shoulder. "I was kidding about that."

"I wasn't. I see it as a challenge."

"Do you like challenges?" she asked softly.

The total darkness of the room added an extra layer of intimacy to their words. The hushed tones, the feeling that they were the only two people in the world, added to his sense of emotional vulnerability.

And to the sense of anything goes.

With that in mind, he figured this was the perfect time to convince Zoe to play his fantasy game.

Shifting on the bed, Dex unerringly found the side-table drawer-pull in the dark. He tugged the drawer open and pulled out the goodies he'd hid there.

"Toys?" she asked. He noted she sounded teasing, not grossed out. Something to keep in mind in the future.

"Something I thought went well with your dominatrix outfit," he told her.

"Um, you realize that was just a costume, right? And a mistaken one at that? I'm not really into…" Her voice trailed off as he pressed the leather restraints in her hand. "Oh, my."

"The leather is soft," he told her, running her fingers along the pliable beltlike length. "It'll wrap around your wrists and the posts of the headboard."

"Why not around *your* wrists?" she joked.

The idea of being completely at her mercy, his body spread out for her to have her way with, made Dex groan.

"Next time," he promised, hoping reverently that there would be another night for these leather straps.

Unable to see in the dark, he trailed his hand up the length of her arm until he found her hand again. He took one of the straps and, shifting so he was angled across her body, wrapped it around the bedpost.

Then he reached for her hand.

He felt her suck in a deep breath, her body going stiff.

"I want to see you," he told her, his fingers tracing a gentle design over her wrist. "I want to drive you crazy in every way I know how. And I want complete control. I want to do things to your body, to touch you and taste you and make you scream in ecstasy."

He felt her excited shudder.

"I'll put the blindfold back on," she offered. "I'm just not sure about the restraints."

"Do you trust me?" he asked quietly.

Long seconds ticked by. A rivulet of sweat ran down Dex's spine. His heart froze as he waited for her answer.

Finally, "Yes," she whispered.

Dex's heart fell. No longer his, he kissed it goodbye, even knowing there was little to no chance she'd give hers in return. It didn't matter, he realized. He'd loved her since they were kids. And now he could show her how much.

Without urging from him, she raised her hand and, finding his, laid it in the leather strap. Dex's breath shuddered, his body tightened.

"Will you stand up?" he asked.

"You're just full of demands, aren't you?" She gave a helpless laugh, the movement making her breasts brush deliciously against his chest. Unable to help himself, Dex slid down and took one nipple into his mouth, suckling the round peak.

Zoe's free hand tunneled through his hair, holding his head there as she arched her back to press her breast deeper into his mouth. He scraped his teeth over the turgid tip, making her gasp, then moan her delight.

He worked her breast, reveling in her delicious response. Finally, he needed more.

"I need you to get up," he murmured, before his tongue traced more tight circles around her areola.

"Isn't that my line?"

"Sweetheart, around you I'm always up," he parried, pressing her free hand to his hard dick in proof.

"Mmm, nice," she complimented him with a squeeze of approval.

He grinned, then shifted, sliding off the side of the bed and standing with his hand still meshed with hers. Her fingers clenched his before she let go. Then he heard her shift over the bedcover and the soft thud of her bare feet on the carpet and the brush of her bare, silky skin against his body as she joined him.

"No spanking," she told him with a breathless laugh.

Dex grinned. Then he turned her around, so she faced the post, and wrapped the other restraint around her free wrist. He slid her wrists, bound by the leather, up to the notch just below the large knob on the bedpost, anchoring them there, just above shoulder height.

"Okay?" he asked.

"Mmm," she murmured. He could tell that she wasn't sure, but was willing to give him a chance.

That's all he needed.

Ever since she was sixteen and had got the angel wings tattoo between her shoulder blades, he'd fantasized about this. He couldn't see the tattoo in the dark, but his mind could trace it perfectly.

First he pressed a kiss to the side of her neck, right where it curved into her shoulder. Then Dex dropped to his knees behind her, running his hands down the smooth, satin skin of her thighs. He shifted her just a little, so her legs were spread wide.

He kissed the vulnerable, tender skin behind her knees, then worked his way up her inner thighs. He could feel her tremble, her legs shaking as he pressed his finger between her thighs and traced her swollen, damp lips.

He pinched her clit, making her shudder and gasp. Then he slid one finger into her, swirling it in time to the subtle shifting of her hips.

Her scent washed over him, engulfing him. Dex had never wanted anything, anyone, the way he wanted Zoe.

He pressed an openmouthed kiss to the small of her back, slowly rising, kissing his way up her spine until he reached the spot that he knew was covered by the angel's wings. His hand worked her; the other reached around to test the weight of her breast, heavier because she was bending slightly. He cupped, squeezed. She murmured her approval.

Then she tried to kill him by pressing her hips against his straining dick. Dex groaned, releasing her briefly to grab a condom off the table and sheath himself. He reached around, using both hands to play her nipples to a fever pitch, using her breathing as his cue.

When her pants turned to gasps, he made his move.

First he pressed just the tip of his dick in, then slid it out. Teased her clit. Pressed it in again.

She moaned, her hips moving in supplication.

"Now," she groaned.

"Not yet," he said, his eyes closed as he teased her again. He could feel the orgasm building inside himself. The image of how they must look filled his mind. He visualized himself standing behind her, her arms strapped to the post and that delicate tattoo clearly outlined on her gorgeous back. In his mind's eye, he saw the curve of her spine, the sweet swell of her buttocks. And his body, poised over her as she begged him.

"Please," she murmured.

That soft word, the breathy tone, broke Dex's control. With a guttural groan, he thrust into her wet, slick flesh. He set a slow, measured pace, building, amping up the sensations. In spite of the blackness of the room, he closed his eyes, letting the feelings take him higher.

Zoe met his thrusts with her own, encouraging him to go deeper, harder.

The pace intensified. In, out. Faster.

He was so close.

One hand was still working her nipples, tweaking and twisting the swollen flesh; the other trailed down between her legs to work her damp clitoris.

He traced the swollen flesh in time with his thrusts. Zoe's breath came quicker and quicker as she twisted and turned, trying to find relief but unable to move her hands because of the restraints.

"Ohmygod, ohmygod, ohmygod," she panted, her words coming out as a gasping cry, growing higher, keener as she arched her back. She pressed her legs against him, tightening her thighs and holding him prisoner as her hips undulated to a faster, more urgent rhythm.

Dex quickened his pace. Unable to keep up the sex play, he slid his hand from between her legs and pressed it against the small of her back. That was the only request she needed. Zoe shifted, bending over just a little more. Dex grabbed her hips, holding tightly as he pounded his way to heaven.

One thrust, then two. Zoe's pants shifted to cries of pleasure. Her body tightened, her inner muscles convulsing. That was all it took to send Dex over the edge.

The world exploded in a colorful prism of stars behind Dex's eyes. He thought he shouted, but wasn't sure since his entire being had coalesced into a throbbing chasm of pleasure. Panting, he struggled to regulate his breath.

Zoe shifted, her body straightening as she leaned against the bedpost and gasped. Dex forced his knees not to buckle. He shifted, aligned his body with hers and laid his head against her back.

He released her hips and slid his hands down her damp, trembling body. In a part breathless, part triumphant tone, he declared, "That's five."

"WE NEVER GOT TO try out my leather," Zoe murmured two hours later as she curled into his arms. Her voice drooped with fatigue and her body tingled in exhausted pleasure. They'd made love two more times, once in the shower and again on the floor on their way out of the shower. Leather be damned, she didn't think she could go another round if he'd promised her a chocolate-covered quadruple orgasm.

She could see hints of light trying to peek through the heavy window coverings and realized it must be dawn. They'd made love five times and while he hadn't managed two dozen orgasms, it hadn't been for lack of trying.

"I think you dominated me just fine without it," he teased, his voice deep with exhaustion. One hand curved over her hip, holding her in place while the other rubbed slow, sleepy circles over the small of her back.

Zoe smiled against his shoulder, her pride sparking with a hint of triumph. Go her, she'd worn out the masked hunk.

"Dex?" she murmured.

"Yeah, sweetheart?"

She waited. She counted thirteen seconds before he went concrete-stiff, all evidence of exhaustion evaporating. His hand froze. So did his breath. Then he cursed.

"How long?" he finally asked in the same tone a guy on death row would use asking for his execution date.

"Since the tree house."

He was quick. With a groan, he realized, "My phone?"

"Yep."

The silence was electric. She could almost hear his brain whirling, questions and defenses aligning, then realigning.

"Are you pissed?"

Zoe had to smile. Leave it to Dex to get right to the point. No excuses, no bullshit. Just immediate damage assessment. She considered his question. Really considered it, trying to pull her brain out of the sexual fog it'd been wrapped in since that night in the garden.

Pissed? No. Confused? A little. Anxious to see what this did to their relationship and where things would go from here? Unquestionably.

"I'm here, aren't I?" she finally said. "Did I feel pissed when I went down on you?"

She felt his laugh more than heard it. A quick move of his chest, a puff of breath against her hair.

"Well, you didn't use your teeth, so that'd have to be a no.

And that'd have to do for now. Because as much as she'
love to debate the ins and outs of everything, her body an
her brain were completely exhausted.

With a tired half smile, Zoe snuggled deeper into Dex'
arms and waited.

Apparently getting that she really wasn't angry, De
heaved a sigh so deep it ruffled her hair. Then he wrapped hi
arms tighter around her in a hug.

"I wasn't screwing with you," he said quietly. She coul
hear the regret, the worry in his tone. And knowing Dex a
well as she did, she knew it was real. "I was just afraid."

Afraid? Zoe's heart, already his, gave a little sigh. Mayb
she was justifying. Maybe she was a little brain-dead afte
wallowing in the best sex of her life. Whatever it was, sh
wanted to believe him. After all, how could she be angr
with a guy who went to such lengths to be with her? She'
never had anyone want her like Dex did. She'd neve
wanted anyone like she did him. He was her fantasy guy
He was the one to make all her sexual dreams come true
it was just perfect.

But still, her insecurities forced her to ask, "What were yo
afraid of?"

He hesitated.

"I was worried I'd ruin our friendship," he finally sai
in a low tone that told her how hard it was for him to adm
it. "Ruin the memories of what we'd had, or worse, not b
able to compete with your memories of me as a nerd
dork."

Zoe couldn't help but laugh.

"But I was a nerdy dork, too," she reminded him.

"You were gorgeous. Sexy, unique, self-possessed," he argued.

Shock left her speechless. He'd really seen her that way? She gave a little sigh and shook her head.

"Later," he continued his confession, "I was worried that you'd get pissed. That you'd think I'd been trying to trick you when I dressed up and didn't tell you who I really was. Or that once you knew, you'd…well, reject me."

"Why would I reject you?" she said, trying to reconcile in her mind that such a strong, sexy guy could have insecurities just as she did.

Even as she asked, a part of her, that tiny mistrusting voice in the back of her head, warned that there was more to this. There had to be. The voice mocked that no guy was going to worry that much about her rejecting him. But for once, Zoe didn't listen to the doubts. She trusted Dex.

Still, she raised her head off his chest and peered at him in the dark. She couldn't see anything, but it made her feel stronger, even as the blackness made it easier to confess, "I get that. Rejection sucks. I feel as though I've been running from it all my life. First from dealing with it. Then later, to prevent it from happening."

She paused, then put her heart out there in a way that terrified and exhilarated her. "Except with you. I trust you, Dexter."

"I'll never give you another reason not to," he assured her, making her smile in delight when he pressed a kiss against her hair. He was just so damned sweet.

"Good," she murmured as exhaustion finally overtook her. "We're good. Just as long as you don't lie to me anymore, of course. I've never trusted anyone like I trust you. If you tell me there are no more secrets, that's all I need."

His arms stiffened against her back. Dex made a sound lo
in his throat. But Zoe fell asleep before her mind could regist
his discomfort.

12

NOT CARING THAT SHE was in the inn lobby, Zoe curled her feet under her and settled into the cushions of the comfy couch in the corner. Her body was still warm and loose from an all-night pleasure-fest, but she wished her mind was a little less foggy. If she'd been thinking straight, she'd have let her phone go to messages instead of rolling over to answer it this morning.

But she had answered, so here she was. Whatever news Brad Young had deemed vital enough that she had to meet him here right after lunch had better be good. Not that she'd be much of a judge, Zoe thought with a sigh. She was operating on about three hours' sleep.

She tapped her fingers in an impatient rhythm on the edge of the small side table. She shifted a little in her chair and gave a hum of pleasure as muscles, not used to such vigorous workout, reminded her of last night.

When she'd wakened in her own bed this morning, the sunlight warming her satisfied body, she hadn't remembered getting back to her room. Had Dex carried her, or had she wandered her naked self on down the hall in a fog of sexual satisfaction?

Before she could do more than wonder about that now, her cell phone rang.

"Hi, Meghan," she answered, smothering a yawn.

"Hey, girly, how's the reunion?"

She glanced around the lobby, noting faces that now had names smiling her way. Two people actually waved. Another sent her a thumbs-up sign. For the first time, Zoe felt like part of a group—felt as though she belonged. And she kinda liked it.

She'd been so upset about the queen nomination last night, sure it was a setup to humiliate her, that she'd run off before she could hear the career hints they'd promised to announce. Tonight was the big event, the unveiling of everyone's real careers and the crowning of the king and queen.

"Apparently, the reunion is pretty good," she said, realizing it actually was. She'd met people like Julie. She'd participated in a few events in the name of asking about Gandalf. People hadn't been disdainful or dismissive, but had actually seemed to enjoy hanging out with her. And she'd enjoyed them, too. When a few had suggested keeping in touch—something Zoe had never thought to do with anyone from high school—she'd even agreed.

"We'll do dinner next week and you can tell me about it," Meghan said. Her words were rushed, as though she was trying to get the social niceties out of the way before she launched into something major.

"Look, I've found out almost every secret this town has to tell," Zoe said quickly. "There's still a chance that it's Brad Young, but he's playing the tease card. I can tell he wants me to keep asking, but I really don't think it's him. Honestly, I'm ninety-nine percent sure that Gandalf isn't at the reunion. But that doesn't mean I'm giving up. It might be Teresa, and she's going to be here tonight for the party. I'll scope her out, okay?" Zoe winced a little. Hopefully Teresa's high-school crush was a thing of the past.

"Hang on," Meghan said slowly, her tone taking on the air of someone about to break bad news. Zoe cringed. "Just forget the Gandalf idea, okay? It was crazy to begin with."

She almost dropped the phone. Fumbling to put it back to her ear, Zoe asked, "Sorry? We must have a bad connection."

"Zach took the job with Microsoft," Meghan said baldly.

Guilt beat on Zoe's shoulders like a hailstorm, pounding home how badly she'd let her brother down. Sure she'd paid lip service to finding Gandalf, but she'd spent most of her time mooning over Dex. Chasing Dex. Doing Dex.

God, she sucked.

"Tell him not to accept yet, please. Give me another day. Or better yet," she said, the image of her laptop lover flashing through her mind. "I might have someone else. Someone even better."

"Zoe—"

"No," she cut her off. "Just wait until I call back, okay? I think I have the perfect person. Give me an hour. Two at the most."

It could work. She'd ask Dex how he'd found an avatar that looked like her when he'd sent her that cyber-sex program. He'd said he had an inside track with Avigraph. Maybe he could introduce her. The possibility swirled in her head.

Not wanting to waste any time explaining, Zoe muttered a quick goodbye, hung up and tossed her phone in her purse. She needed to find Dex. She headed toward the reception desk to have him paged. Before she'd taken five steps, someone grabbed her shoulder.

She turned, ready to brush off whoever it was and saw Brad's leering face.

"Zoe, I missed you last night," he greeted her, pulling her into a tight hug.

She grimaced against his broad chest, then pushed away.

"I was busy," she said, mentally rolling her eyes at how apropos that statement was. "Look, I'm sorry to do this, but I have to run. There's someone I need to talk to."

"Did you hear the news?" he said, his brown eyes sparkling with amusement and something that looked like malice. "They made the big announcement."

He dropped his arm around her shoulder, pulling her so close his thigh pressed against hers. Weirded out, Zoe tried to duck away without making a big deal of it. She didn't know why, but Brad was making her feel as though there wasn't enough air in the room. Smothered, almost.

"Kiss your king, sweetheart," he said, pulling her into another hug.

Zoe didn't bother to play nice this time. She shoved her palms against his chest and pushed away. "Congratulations," she said with a stiff smile. "I've got to go, though."

Apparently he expected more accolades than that. The physical kind. His smile took on a nasty edge. "Don't you want to hear who's queen?"

"Not really." She figured Candice was still in the banquet hall gloating over her crown. Other than feeling bad for Julie, she didn't care.

"Look, I really have to go," she said, pulling away again. "There's someone I need to talk to."

"I'm the guy you want." His smile was cheesy, his eyes hard. Zoe realized in that moment that she'd been a complete and total idiot as a teenager.

She shook her head and turned to leave.

"I hear you've been asking all over and now that you've got me, you're gonna walk?"

She frowned and glanced at him over her shoulder.

"I'm Gandalf. Keep it to yourself, though," he said in a jovial, almost political tone. "I hear you've been asking questions, trying to find me."

Zoe turned to face him fully. He was saying the right words, but her lie detector was working overtime. Between her and Julie, they'd talked to everyone and all but ruled Brad out. Not because the evidence didn't point to him—what little there was did—but because the original game had a strong, kick-ass heroine and the reality was that Brad was a misogynistic pig. That, and while she hadn't found out what his actual job was, she knew he'd been living in Texas and that his work had something to do with engineering. Not computers. So why would he make it up?

"Let's go somewhere and talk privately, okay? I don't want my, you know, identity getting out."

Brad's gaze flicked to the side, his face hardening at whatever he saw over Zoe's shoulder. She was about to glance back to see for herself, but before she could, he grabbed her hand and pulled her to her feet.

"C'mon, babe. Let's head up to my hotel room. We'll have all the privacy we want there," Brad persuaded, trying to move her toward the elevators.

Zoe twisted away and shot him a puzzled look. "Your room? You're kidding, right? We're private enough here."

An ugly look flashed across his face, then he shrugged and gave her that patented good-ol'-boy smile. "You know what I mean. We're a team now, right? You want my help, I want a little something from you."

Zoe's jaw dropped. He was serious? Anger bubbled to the surface, but she shoved it back down. Misogynistic pig or not, if he *was* telling the truth, her brother wanted to talk to this jerk. In one piece, which meant she couldn't rip his head off until after Zach decided if he wanted him or not.

"I wanted to talk to you about Gandalf designing a video game for my brother's company," she snapped. "Not about running off to your room to relive a failed high-school rendezvous."

"Then you're talking to the wrong guy."

Zoe gasped and turned to see Dex standing behind her. Brad's glare turned uglier.

"I'd say she's talking to the right guy," Brad snapped, grabbing her arm again. "She's with the guy she chose, loser. Get over it."

"Hey," Zoe protested, tugging her arm away from Brad. "Cut the crap."

While the idea of two guys fighting over her might be ego-stroking, feeling once more like a bone between two snarling dogs wasn't.

"C'mon, Zoe," Brad urged. "You need my help, right?"

"No." She shook her head. She was sure she'd been right before. Brad wasn't Gandalf. "I don't believe you're the guy to help me."

"Listen to her," Dex taunted quietly. "I warned you that you'd lose. Cheating won't change anything."

What the hell were they talking about?

A couple of people stopped as well, surreptitiously watching while pretending not to. Perfect way to ruin her happy morning-after glow. A public scene. Zoe's shoulders tensed, her lifelong issue with being watched and judged urging her to throw her hands in the air and walk away.

But this was Dex. Still, glancing between the two men, if

she had to choose between Brad, the biggest jerk in the world, and Dex, who was suddenly flexing his ego annoyingly, she'd have to take Dex. After all, she knew he had other things that flexed much better.

The few onlookers were now a dozen. At this point, they weren't even pretending not to watch the confrontation. Whispered conversations scurried around the three of them like scampering mice.

Zoe wanted to writhe in embarrassment. It was high school all over again. She shifted toward Dex.

"Did you tell your girlfriend where her nickname came from, computer boy?" Brad called out before she could take a step.

"Don't," Dex warned, his tone low and threatening.

Zoe's frown deepened. What did Dex have to do with that nickname? She looked at the gathered crowd, the nods and whispers, and realized they all knew something she didn't. Her stomach clenched into a vicious knot. Her shoulders automatically stiffened and her chin lifted to show them she didn't care.

"Mr. Big Shot here is the guy behind your virgin tagline back in school," Brad accused.

Zoe shook her head in denial. Dex wouldn't do that. Brad gestured to the clump of people. She followed his gaze and saw the nods.

Her gaze flew to Dex's face. He set his jaw and gave a disgusted shake of his head. She wasn't sure if he was denying the accusation, or if it was guy code for a warning to kick Brad's ass for spilling a secret.

The room spun. Zoe's mind spun with it. Dex? But she trusted him. She saw Candice edge her way through the crowd, a malicious smile on her face. Fury buried Zoe's confusion in a quick wave. How could Dex turn her into a public spectacle like this?

He grabbed her arm. Zoe gasped and tried to shake him off. The hell he'd top off her embarrassment by dragging her off like a Neanderthal. But he didn't let her loose.

"Dex," she hissed.

Humiliation took hold as he ignored her.

Past Brad's gloating face and the gathering crowd of curious faces, he pulled Zoe over to the registration desk, around and into the small staff room.

Two bellboys and a concierge stared in shock.

"Out," he commanded.

They scattered.

Zoe wasn't as easily intimidated, though. She held tight to the fury, needing it to keep the pain at bay. She slammed her arms across her chest, cocked one hip to the side and glared.

"Who the hell do you think you are, dragging me around like that?" she challenged, anger over the spectacle battling with humiliation over his high-handed arrogance.

"You were using me," he accused as soon as he'd slammed the door shut. "Did you know all along? Was this just some game to you?"

"Using you?" She shook her head, trying to make sense of his accusation. "How the hell was I using you?"

"You knew I was under the mask before you slept with me," he accused, his face twisted in anger. "Did you know I was Gandalf, too? Is that why you agreed to our night together?"

Zoe stepped back. Her legs hit the desk, the tiny room closed in, trapping her. Her head spun. Everything went blurry as the words hit her like a bomb. "You're Gandalf?"

He'd lied to her. She'd asked him. Twice, she'd asked. And he'd lied. Just like he'd lied last night. Zoe reached blindly behind her, finding a chair and falling into it. She could barely wrap her mind around the facts slapping her in the face. Facts she should have known deep down. Facts she'd obviously ignored in some idiotic need to believe him.

Zoe gasped, pain cutting deep gouges in her heart. Her breath shuddered as she tried to gather her thoughts, grabbing on to anger in self-defense.

"*You* lied to *me*," she accused. "If hiding behind a mask wasn't enough, you lied on top of it. I knew it was crazy to get involved with you. But I thought it was because it'd ruin our friendship. Instead I find out we don't even have a friendship."

"That's bullshit."

"Is it? You lied to me, Dexter. You hid your identity, you lied about your job." Her voice broke, but she couldn't stop the words from pouring out in a pained whisper. "You humiliated me."

She wanted to yell at him for breaking her heart. For making her believe she could count on him, that she could trust him. But Zoe couldn't even put that betrayal into words. The pain, the misery poured from her heart like blood, seeping all around her as that little voice in her head taunted, *I told you so.*

"I humiliated you?" he asked in an ironic tone. "You used me, Zoe. I thought you accepted me. Just me, for myself. But like all those assholes out there, you wanted something from me and didn't hesitate to justify your actions to get it."

She just stared. She had wanted his friendship. His body. And stupid her, his love. But he was wrong. She hadn't used him. Not the way he meant. And if he believed she had, that she was no better than those parasites who'd always made him feel like a walking wallet, then that proved he didn't care for her. It proved he didn't even know her.

Zoe stepped toward the door.

"What are you doing?"

"Leaving," she told him.

"Without resolving this?" he asked with a stunned shake of his head. "Just like you walk away from anything that forces you to stand up and defend your actions? Is anything worth fighting for, Zoe? Or will you always run away?"

The truth hurt. But no more than his betrayal. So she lifted her chin, gave him her patented glare of disdain and latched on to her only weapon. Brad's pathetic lie.

"Relationship?" she taunted. "That'd be this little thing between us that consists of lies, a mask and that ugly moniker you slapped on me ten years ago?"

Zoe's heart stopped at the look of guilt on his suddenly white face. Oh, God. She'd just said that to get out of the room. But he'd really had something to do with it?

"Just like your actual identity, you didn't think I'd ever find out about that lie either, did you?" she asked. Suddenly, the fight drained from her, leaving a pained, empty shell. One that was in imminent danger of collapsing.

Needing privacy before it happened, Zoe stepped away from Dex. Blindly, she found the door handle and wrenched it open. Ignoring the crowd, she headed for the elevators.

"Where are you going?" he demanded, catching up to her.

"I'm done," she said, pressing the up button.

"Well, I'm not," he said, grabbing her arm.

Zoe shook his hand off. "No touching. I don't want you near me," she demanded. She couldn't take not knowing she'd never feel his hands on her again. "If I'm done, we're done."

"Just like you to walk away," he muttered.

Too empty to defend herself, Zoe just shrugged. "You'd know. You've never done anything to stop me."

With that, she lifted her chin, wrapped the remnants of her pride around her like a cloak and stepped into the elevator.

"Goodbye," she murmured as the doors closed.

FIVE MINUTES AFTER he'd watched Zoe's tearstained face disappear into the elevator, Dex flexed his sore fist as he stared down at Brad's bruised one on the floor at his feet.

"That's what I should have done ten years ago when you messed with Zoe the first time," Dex stated as the jerk struggled back to his feet.

"Dude, hitting me isn't going to change the fact that you lost. You lost the girl." Brad flexed his jaw from side to side and shrugged to show he didn't care. But his fists clenched at his sides and he balanced on the balls of his feet in a way that told Dex he was biding his time. "You know, just like in school, once your usefulness was over, nobody gave a rat's ass about you."

Dex didn't even bother using his fist this time. He shoved the idiot hard. Brad fell backward into a tall oak pedestal, sending a vase of autumn flowers crashing to the floor in wet, sloppy chaos.

Just great. His mother loved that damned vase. Breathing hard, Dex glared at the mess. He had to get out of here. Had to find a place to think, regroup. He pushed his way through the crowd.

"That looked like one of the moves from *Class Warfare: The Takedown*."

Perfect. He had thought it couldn't possibly get any worse. Dex hung his head as shame washed over him, and he turned to face his grandmother.

It only took a few words, some stern looks and a swat of the velvet case carrying her tarot cards to disperse the crowd.

"Sorry about the mess," he muttered, kicking at the broken vase with the toe of his shoe. Then her words sank in. His head shot up and he gave her a quizzical look. "How would you know what the move was from? I didn't think you even knew the name of my last game?"

"Don't be a schmuck, Dexter," Essie said, making a sweeping motion with her hand to indicate to the bellboy to come clean up the shards of pottery. Then she tucked her hand into Dex's arm and, with strength he hadn't realized she had, tugged him out the door. "Your father and I play all the time. Your mother tries, but bless her heart, she has no hand-eye coordination."

Dex just stared. The words only added to the surreal night-mare quality of his afternoon.

Obviously sensing he didn't want to talk about his mother's gaming skills, his grandma sighed and patted his arm. "You and that other man were fighting over Zoe?"

"Not over her," Dex clarified. "More like about her."

It wasn't like the winner got her as their prize. Or that she'd ever have anything to do with either of them again. That didn't take away a single iota of the satisfaction Dex felt remember-ing Brad's face after it'd encountered his fist.

It all spun in his head. Zoe had used him. She'd believed Brad. She really thought Dex had made up that obnoxious virgin moniker. After everything they'd had together, all they'd shared. Dex hadn't realized he could hurt like this.

"She's a sweet girl, but she didn't seem the type to want anyone fighting over—or *about*—her."

"She used me," Dex muttered.

"Oh, Dexter," his grandmother admonished in disgust. "Jump off the pity wagon already."

Good God, not her, too. Too numb even to feel shock, he stared down at his lifelong champion. She rolled her eyes, then let go of his arm to take a seat on the garden bench.

"You have never in your life done a single thing against your will."

He opened his mouth to rattle off his list, but before he could utter a syllable, she shook her head. "Don't confuse people thinking they were using you with the actual thing. You have always seen through games. You've twisted them to your advantage if they interested you. Ignored them if they didn't."

"Maybe," he admitted with a frown as he considered what her words really meant. Did that make him as big a jerk as he'd always considered the people using him?

"And this girl called you on it, didn't she?"

"She called me things, all right," he muttered under his breath. But his grandma's words started to sink in. Dex hunched his shoulders against the cold and looked out over the golden fields of autumn grass.

He really was a schmuck. What had he had to lose by telling Zoe about Gandalf? Hiding behind anonymity was stupid. He'd known all along she wanted to talk to him. If he'd just let go of his need to be wanted for himself, his paranoia about being used, he could have settled it all a long time ago.

Just as he'd worn the mask to hide from Zoe's rejection, he'd found an excuse to hide from giving her a chance to want him for himself.

"You love her."

Dex shoved his hands in his pockets with a frown. He wanted to deny it. He wanted it not to be true. Love—it sucked. It hurt. But even as miserable as it felt to remember the pain in Zoe's green eyes when she'd told him to get out of her life, he couldn't stop his feelings. Hell, he hadn't been able to after ten years away from her. What made him think that pissing her off, publicly humiliating her and ruining their chances together would stop them?

He was such an ass. Turning, he headed back toward the lobby.

"Where do you think you're going?"

He stopped and gave his grandmother a sheepish smile.

"I'm going to talk to Zoe. I need to tell her how I feel."

"No."

"What?" Shocked, Dex spun around to stare at his grandmother. "Why wouldn't I tell her? This is important, isn't it? Women want to hear that kind of thing."

"If you wanted to tell her, you'd have said it already. Telling her now is just another way of trying to manipulate the situation, Dexter. This isn't a game you can strategize your way through. You have to let her make her own choices."

"She needs all of the information to make those choices." He shifted toward the inn again. He wanted to talk to her. Had to talk to her. Now, before she left. He knew Zoe; she was probably already packed and ready to run.

"Then you should have given her that information up front, shouldn't you?" came the dry admonishment.

Dex clenched his teeth to hold back the ugly flow of curses. He'd never sworn in front of his grandma and he wasn't about to start now.

She stared calmly back, looking like a tiny Mrs. Claus who'd just put his name on the naughty list. "Leave her be, Dexter. She needs time and space to sort things out."

"What if she takes off?"

There, he said it. Voiced his biggest fear—that Zoe would

leave him. Again. That she'd use her anger to ignore what they'd had together, to fall back on her mistrust of him—justified or not—and cut him out of her life.

"If she leaves, then it wasn't meant to be," his grandma intoned, as sagely as if she'd just flipped the death card across the table.

He thought of that poem his mom used to have on a plaque in the hallway. Something about loving things and letting them go. He'd always thought that was pure crap.

But he couldn't tell his grandma that. Not when she was giving him the evil eye. Instead, he just shrugged as though he was agreeing.

Instead, he was already figuring his strategy. He had Zoe's address. He had her brother's company name. He could track her down. If she left before he could fix things, he'd just have to hunt her down and make her his.

13

"You're not going to let them win, are you?"

She'd tried hiding in her room, but pride, hunger and the memories of Dex had finally driven her out. Now, focused on burying her misery with the entire pan of caramel dutch apple pie in front of her, Zoe barely flicked Julie a glance.

Until the other woman plopped herself down in the chair across from her.

"What the...?" This friend thing was turning into a pain in the ass.

"Don't give them the satisfaction," Julie commanded, her blue eyes concerned, her face set in determined lines.

"I don't want to talk," Zoe said, focusing her tear-reddened eyes on the pie.

"Brad lied, you know."

"I have a brain, don't I? Of course I know he lied."

At least about being Gandalf. But the rest? Zoe didn't know what to think. The guilt on Dex's face was hard to argue with. Not able to deal with it yet, Zoe stabbed viciously at an apple slice.

"You don't sound like you believe it, though." Julie waited for a response, then, apparently giving up the fight, she grabbed the fork on her side of the table and scooped up a bite of Zoe's pie.

Zoe shrugged. She'd been so devastated to realize Dex had lied to her—not once but twice—about Gandalf, she hadn't paid much attention to Brad's assertion. Everyone else apparently had, though.

"Dex didn't come up with that title," Zoe stated with a grimace. "But he had something to do with it."

"Zoe, I was there when Brad first said it," Julie admitted. "Dex wasn't anywhere around."

Zoe frowned at her caramelized apple. She'd seen guilt on his face. Had she been wrong? Did it matter? One lie or two, he'd still deceived her.

"You're sure?" God, she was pathetic.

"Yep, totally sure." Apparently figuring she needed sustenance after her confession, Julie helped herself to another forkful of apple pie. "But you sure gave Brad a cheap thrill thinking he conned you into believing he did. Almost made up for the fact that he lost his bet about getting you into bed."

Zoe rolled her eyes, finally understanding Brad's push to get her into his room. It seemed some things never change.

"Apparently he couldn't handle not being the biggest deal out of Central High. He was jealous of all the rumors about Gandalf. He didn't think the real guy would show, so he tried to fool everyone into thinking *he* was the wizard—hence the costume. When he heard you were poking around about this Gandalf, he figured he'd con you, too. Of course, Dex took care of him," Julie said with a wicked laugh as she licked flaky pie crust off her thumb. "He punched Brad in the face. Right there, in front of everyone."

Zoe gaped. Julie gave a beatific smile. "It was so sweet."

It *was* sweet. Zoe's heart did a little tumble, the ache of betrayal fading as she fought her way through her trust issues to realize that Dex, of all people, wouldn't betray her. So what was behind his Gandalf lie? He had to have had a reason. But she hadn't given him a chance to share it, had she? Nope, she'd launched into her mistrustful defense mode, lashed out and kicked him to the curb before he could reject her.

Damn, she was smart.

"Was Brad behind nominating me for queen?" Zoe asked, trying to connect all the dots.

Julie shook her head. "Nope. That was Candice. I think she figured it'd pit us against each other. Ruin our budding friendship."

Typically, Zoe had jumped to the immediate conclusion that the nomination had been some trick to humiliate her and had walked out. She was starting to see a pattern here.

"Did it?" Zoe found herself holding her breath as she waited for the answer.

"Only if I gain twenty pounds because of this pie."

Zoe grinned.

"Candice has spent the past twelve hours begging Brad to stay in touch with her, promising people the moon in exchange for their vote and chasing Dex's grandma trying to get her to read her cards." The words were flat, the pity clear on Julie's face. "She's not a threat to you, Zoe. She never has been. She's just kind of sad."

Zoe followed Julie's nod, noting the blonde sitting at a corner table alone, nursing a cup of coffee.

She seemed deflated. Instead of the evil cause of all that had been wrong in Zoe's teenage life, Candice was just a woman. A woman who looked as though life hadn't rocked so much after high school. Zoe stared at the blonde for a long moment.

Then she sighed and, as much as the immature, bitchy side of her hated to do it, she let go of her teenage resentments.

"Maybe we should send her over a piece of pie?" she mused.

Julie stared at her, the last caramel apple slice falling unnoticed off her fork. "You're kidding, right? Why would you do that?"

Because Zoe'd come to realize she had to take risks if she ever wanted to have anything worth holding on to? Because keeping people at arm's length wasn't working anymore? Because sooner or later she had to risk letting people get to know her, and the first step to that was getting to know them?

"Because you took a chance and befriended me. I can't tell you what a difference that's made for me. It's only fair that I pay the favor forward. Besides, maybe it's time for all of us to grow up," Zoe finally said, pulling her big-girl panties on.

And what d'ya know? They fit.

DEX STARED AT HIS laptop screen, his mind blank. He'd never had this happen before. Like impotence, it was one of those rumored things that only happened to other guys.

But here he was. Empty. Blank. No ideas for getting Zoe back. No strategy to play the game. Nothing.

He slapped the laptop closed and pushed away from the kitchen table. Maybe that was the problem. He'd thought of it as a game. Which put Zoe on the opposing team. Stupid, since he knew he couldn't win without her by his side.

That'd been his mistake from the beginning, he realized. Trying to play her. To use games and strategy instead of just being up-front and honest. All because…what? He was afraid? What a freaking wimp.

To hell with orders to stay in the house. He needed to see Zoe.

Dex turned toward the phone, not even willing to waste the time of walking over to the inn to see if she was still registered.

In mid-turn, he stopped cold. His heart rapped against his chest, and he had to force himself not to rub his eyes. Like a dream, there she stood, in a long, black trench coat and those sexy boots.

"I haven't seen you at the inn," Zoe said as if she hadn't just strolled uninvited into his parents' house and startled the hell out of him. Her smile was friendly, but her eyes were sharp. She might be playing nice, but she hadn't forgotten his betrayal.

That was okay with him, though. He'd take her any way he could get her. Just as long as she gave him a chance to talk. To explain. Hell, given that there was no explanation, he'd settle for groveling.

"I'm grounded," he told her, only half joking. "My grandma decided I needed to cool off and have some thinking time. I'm pretty sure she just wanted to make sure I didn't pick any more fights in the lobby."

"Oh, I don't know. Your last one was a winner." She shot him a mischievous grin. "You gave Brad Young a fat lip and a nasty black eye."

Dex couldn't stop his gloating smile. But then he looked closer at Zoe and saw the stress on her face, the tense set of her shoulders, and his grin faded.

"Why are you here?" he asked.

"You didn't come to me."

"You told me not to."

"Since when do you do as I tell you?"

"Always," Dex said with a rueful shrug. "I've always tried to do whatever you wanted, Zoe. Whether you realized it or not, all I've ever wanted was for you to be happy."

She smiled. A simple, sweet look that accepted his statement at face value. The deep freeze around Dex's heart melted a little as hope peeked through. His answering smile was filled with relief.

"I'm sorry I lied to you," he said quietly.

She arched one brow, her eyes cautious. He could see the hurt lurking in their green depths. He figured he'd start with the first issue, then move on to the bigger one. "Zoe, I promise, I didn't make up that nickname."

She frowned, obviously having expected him to go straight to the Gandalf issue. Before she could say anything, he forced his words out. "I was behind it, though."

Her mouth dropped open.

"I set up the interruption by his parents that ruined your date with Brad. I was jealous, hated the idea of you going out with him. Anyone, but especially him." Dex shrugged, not sure how to excuse his seventeen-year-old self's idiocy. "I guess he was humiliated by how it all turned out and lashed out. But it was you that got hurt."

Zoe still stared, her eyes huge. Finally, she said, "I can't believe I never noticed you had a thing for me way back in school."

Dex laughed. "I've had a thing for you forever."

She smiled. A tiny, cautious curve of her lips. Hope unfurled in Dex's belly.

"I wasn't using you," she told him quietly.

Dex's smile fell away. Uncomfortable and not sure how to proceed, he shoved his hands into his pockets and shrugged.

"I know you weren't," he said with a sigh. "You didn't hide anything, you didn't play me in any way."

She arched a teasing brow, breaking the tension and making Dex grin. "Okay, you didn't play me in any way I didn't want you to. I'm…" He blew out a frustrated breath and admitted, "…paranoid, I guess. I overanalyze, overstrategize. It's an occupational hazard, I suppose."

"Speaking of…?" She didn't have to say anything else.

"I didn't really lie," he said. Her brows shot up and she shook her head. Then she turned on her heel as if to leave. "Wait. I didn't. I *was* Gandalf. I developed him, I created his games. But I sold the rights, and with them I signed a gag order."

She stopped, glanced over her shoulder to gauge the truth of his words. Dex wanted to protest the doubt, but knew he didn't have a leg to stand on.

Thankfully, he watched her turn back around. The move made her knee-length coat fly open a little at the hem. He got an intriguing glimpse of what he'd swear were fishnet stockings.

Dex's mouth started to water.

"So you're not designing games anymore?" she clarified, pulling his attention away from her knees and the sudden burning need to know what she was wearing under that heavy wool jacket.

"Not as Gandalf," he confirmed. "Leeton owns the rights to those games, the name and persona. But I've started my own company. Still in video-gaming, but I'm expanding. I've got ideas, a lot of connections and want to go out on my own. Avigraph is mine. You saw the prototype. Well, sort of. The system avatars I've designed are usually dressed."

Her green eyes warmed and she tucked a curl behind her ear. Wandering around the kitchen now, she fiddled with the teapot on the stove, then rubbed a flower petal between her fingers. Dex waited, staring and wishing he had X-ray vision.

Wondering what was under that coat was killing him. Just

punishment, he knew she'd say. He'd take whatever chastisement she dished out, as long as he could touch her again. His mouth watered again, as he remembered the taste of her, just there behind the knee as he'd kissed his way up her legs.

He bit back a groan as he remembered everything that had followed that kiss. He pulled his hands from the front pockets of his jeans, the denim material suddenly too tight for comfort.

"I contacted your brother," he told her, that fact suddenly popping into his head through the lusty fog. "I overheard you mention him to Brad and figured, even without the Gandalf tag, maybe I could help him out."

Zoe stopped just a foot away from him, her scent refogging his brain as she stared, her eyes huge. He held his breath when it looked like she was going to reach out and lay her hand on his arm. But she stopped halfway and pulled back to trace a finger over his closed laptop.

"You really called him?"

Trying to bury his frustration, Dex just nodded.

Her smile lit up the room. "Thank you. I appreciate that. He's done so much for me, I really wanted to give him a shot at his dreams."

"Apparently he's closing up shop," Dex clarified. "He said he'd taken a job with one of the big boys. He sounded like he wants that, the security of it. But we're going to get together in a week or so and talk about some side work."

"Really? I love that idea." Zoe's smile was as bright as sunshine. "When I talked to him a couple of hours ago, he sounded relieved. I had no idea how much stress trying to stay afloat was causing him. Turns out he's been thinking of going with Microsoft for a while.

"Actually—" she gave him a naughty little smile

"—Meghan, his wife, started to tell me but I was a little distracted with your sexy virtual message when she was on the phone."

She tapped her finger on his laptop, her words and the reminder flashing images of their wild avatar sex through his brain. Dex wondered what she'd say if he told her he'd saved the video and tortured himself by watching it over and over.

"You were the first one to see that," he explained. "It was a test run of sorts."

"I've never seen anything so intuitively realistic," she commented, running her tongue along her bottom lip. She tapped her fingers over the laptop again, as if reminding him of how hot that cartoon sex had been, then trailed the same fingers down her throat, ending at the collar of her coat. She fiddled with the button, but didn't undo it.

"Thanks." His fingers tingled with the need to touch her. To feel her satiny skin under his hands. This was driving him crazy. He wanted to be done talking business, but realized she was calling the shots here. "It's a take on my new project."

"Is that where you're going with this? Avatar sex clubs?" she teased.

He grinned, amused at the idea. "Nah. I'm not interested in social networks. I'm thinking training applications, maybe something with the military, but with a few new twists and angles."

"Brilliant." Her hand smoothed up and down the placket of her coat now, teasing him with tiny glimpses of bare skin here and there.

"So…" Dex hesitated. How did he put it without pissing her off? Zoe raised a brow and waited. Since he kept getting intriguing little peeks of black leather through the closure of her coat, he didn't make her wait long. "What're the chances that you'd come to work for me?"

She laughed.

Dex frowned. "I wasn't kidding."

Her smile dropped, her laughter fading into silence.

"You don't want me to work with you. Not really."

"But I do. You're smart, you're connected, you've got great ideas. That's one of the things Zach mentioned when we talked, about how you were so ahead of the curve. You have an instinct for what will work and what won't. He said if he'd listened to you, he'd have been a lot better off."

Zoe's face softened, a sweet look of humbled appreciation glistening in her bottle-green eyes.

"We'll negotiate," she said with a smile. "I'll warn you, though, I'm not cheap."

Figuring it was safe now, Dex stepped forward to pull her into his arms. Her hand flew up, palm out. Her smile dropped. She shook her head.

"I don't think so," she said, her voice suddenly taking on a commanding tone. "You've had your say. Now it's my turn."

He'd rather she have her say while he had his hands on her, but she was calling the shots here. Dex shoved his hands into his pockets to keep his itchy fingers from reaching for her. His eyes dropped to her black leather stiletto boots and his heart stopped. He remembered her body, those boots wrapped over his shoulders, and the delicious taste of her.

Maybe she'd talk fast?

Apparently she planned on using body language. Zoe's hands went to the belt on her trench coat. She slowly untied the fabric, then with a flick of her fingers, unbuttoned the jacket. A quick shimmy and it dropped to the floor.

Immediately followed by Dex's jaw.

"Damn," he breathed.

Zoe tugged the riding crop from the waistband of her tiny leather skirt. She used it to trace a tempting trail from her studded choker, over the tip of her leather bra and down to her fishnet-covered knee.

"Whip me, beat me, make me do anything you want," he said reverentially.

Then he saw her unwrap the leather restraints he'd used on her from her wrist. His dick, already hard, stiffened like an iron bar.

Wow, bad-boy fantasies really did come true.

Zoe snickered, remembering him using similar words when he'd first seen her in this costume at the party. Was it less than a week ago? It felt like a lifetime.

Who knew after ten years of pretending to be an adult, she'd actually grow up in only five days? And in her first all-grown-up act, she snapped her riding crop against the counter and ordered, "Bedtime, big boy. Lead the way to your room."

Dex laughed. She brandished the crop again, only this time she used it to trace a seductive path down the front of her leather bikini top and over the straps crisscrossing her belly.

His laughter faded, hunger lighting his aquamarine eyes. He angled his head toward the stairs and said, "After you."

Zoe sashayed up the stairs, the feel of Dex's eyes on her swaying hips a potent aphrodisiac. He gestured to the door on the right and she preceded him into his boyhood bedroom. Her heart melted a little when she saw the various pictures of the two of them taped around his mirror.

But that was the past. And she was here to negotiate the future. Tapping her crop against her thigh, she gestured to the bed. "Take off your shirt, lie down and listen, sugar. Now I'm in charge."

Dex laughed.

Zoe slapped the riding crop against the footboard. The grin slid off his face, a look of intense sexual heat lighting his eyes. His gaze never leaving hers, he flicked the buttons open and dropped his shirt to the floor.

Zoe gave a hum of appreciation at the sight of that gorgeous chest. She'd kissed it, touched it, collapsed against it. But this was the first time she'd actually seen it. Her breath quickened. She wanted this. To see his eyes, to see his face while they made love. While she opened her heart to him.

"So I decided to stick around," she told him as she traced the riding crop down his naked chest. It was hard to concentrate on her plan when he was half-naked in front of her, but she was determined.

"Not for a job, although we can talk about that possibility later." She liked the idea of working with Dex every once in a while. She loved what she did with her consulting gig. But Dex as a home base held a great deal of appeal. And, for the first time ever, she wasn't worried that someone would get sick of her after a few months. After all, she planned on being together with Dex for a good long time.

"You're sticking around here?" Dex asked, his tone distracted as he obeyed the motion of her crop and lay down on the bed.

"I'm sticking around *you*," she said softly. His eyes rounded in pleasure. Zoe cleared the nerves out of her throat and continued in a stronger voice. "I want to be with you. You make me feel so much."

Needing to touch him, she tossed the crop on the dresser and stepped over to the bed. She placed one knee on the bed and hitched the other over his waist to straddle him.

"I'm going to stick around long enough for you to get to know me. The grown-up me, with all my quirks and foibles and flaky habits." Just saying it out loud scared her to death, but Zoe knew it'd be okay. Knew Dex would accept her, flaky foibles and all.

"I love you, Zoe."

She blinked hard and fast, not wanting to remember this moment through a haze of tears. Her gaze clear and strong, her eyes met his and she smiled. She'd thought this would be the hardest thing she'd ever done.

"I love you, too," she said softly. "I love how you make me laugh. I love how you help your parents and you love your grandma. I love your imagination and your brilliant mind."

And it was just that easy. Zoe pressed her hands to his chest and breathed in. Just breathed the joy and happiness that was rushing around her.

"I love how you make me feel."

"Tell me."

"You make me feel strong. Capable. Wanted."

Dex's hands curved over her leather-covered breasts, his eyes closing in delight.

"You know what I'm going to make you feel now, don't you?"

Zoe grinned. Straightening, she arched her back and scraped her nails gently down his chest. "Pleasure?"

"Loved," he promised.

Epilogue

JOSIE SAUNTERED into Dressed to Thrill after lunch and almost tripped over the delivery boxes piled next to the counter. Rubbing her ankle, she tried not to pout. Oh, not over the fact that Carol had left them there for her to put away. That was normal. But this meant that Tom had already been by. Again. While she was gone. This made the fourth time this week.

She kicked at one of the thick cardboard crates. Was he avoiding her? He knew when her lunch was. She'd told him when she'd been hinting around, hoping he'd ask her to eat with him. So what? Now he was delivering when he knew she wasn't going to be around?

"Josie, can you log those returns in?" Carol said as she strode through the front of the shop.

"Sure," Josie said without enthusiasm.

"I sure hope our regular delivery guy is back soon," Carol said as she frowned at the stack of boxes over her bifocals. "He's nice enough to take the delivery to the storeroom for me. This temp driver refused, if you can believe it."

"Tom didn't deliver these?" Josie's heart picked up a beat. Maybe he wasn't avoiding her?

"Tom? That's our regular guy? No, he's apparently training someone on a different route the past week or so."

Her heart reassured, Josie smiled and scooped up as many

boxes as she could carry. She hummed a happy tune as she got to work.

A half hour and a much happier Josie later, she opened the last returned costume and glanced at the manifest. It was supposed to be Betty Boop. She pulled out the leather dominatrix getup and groaned, her happy tune fading away. What had happened? Then she remembered the mix-up. She'd been so flustered thinking that Tom might be flirting with her, she'd sent the wrong costume. Carol was going to chew her out.

She grimaced and let the leather drop back into the box. She knew she should be worried, but it was hard to care. Tom had actually flirted with her, thanks to this costume.

She spied an envelope and frowned. The order had been paid for by credit card, so what was this?

She glanced over her shoulder to make sure Carol wasn't around, then flicked open the envelope.

Dressed to Thrill:

You might want to be a little more careful double-checking your orders. Unless Betty Boop was kinkier than I knew, this was definitely not the costume that was ordered. No harm, though. It actually turned out to be perfect. Something about dressing up in leather and carrying a riding crop pushed me into finding my inner dominatrix and taking control of my life. After all, there's no way a gal can worry about what others think of her when she's commanding this kind of attention. Which led to an amazing reunion, a whole new future and, well, silly as it sounds, true love.

So thanks. And hey, I hope it brings someone else as much luck as it did me.

Zoe Gaston

Josie grinned. Well, well. Maybe these costumes *could* bring a little luck to the wearer. She eyed the leather and decided maybe to try something a little tamer. Maybe a harem outfit, or a space-princess look? She had a great Marilyn Monroe costume here somewhere. Anything but the fluffy bunny suit. She glanced around the shop and let her imagination take over.

Oh, yeah, now she had a plan. She'd start showing off the merchandise. Tom wasn't going to know what hit him.

**We'll be spotlighting a different series
every month throughout 2009
to celebrate our 60th anniversary.**

Look for Silhouette® Nocturne™ in October!

Travel through time to experience tales
that reach the boundaries of life and death.
Bestselling authors Lindsay McKenna, Cindy
Dees, P.C. Cast and Merline Lovelace join
together in a brand-new, four-book
Time Raiders miniseries.

TIME RAIDERS

nocturne™

New York Times bestselling author
and co-author of the House of Night novels

P.C. CAST

makes her stellar debut
in Silhouette® Nocturne™

THE AVENGER

Available October wherever books are sold.

REQUEST YOUR FREE BOOKS!

2 FREE NOVELS PLUS 2 FREE GIFTS!

HARLEQUIN®

Blaze™

Red-hot reads!

YES! Please send me 2 FREE Harlequin® Blaze™ novels and my 2 FREE gifts (gifts are worth about $10). After receiving them, if I don't wish to receive any more books, I can return the shipping statement marked "cancel". If I don't cancel, I will receive 6 brand-new novels every month and be billed just $4.24 per book in the U.S. or $4.71 per book in Canada. That's a savings of 15% off the cover price. It's quite a bargain. Shipping and handling is just 50¢ per book.* I understand that accepting the 2 free books and gifts places me under no obligation to buy anything. I can always return a shipment and cancel at any time. Even if I never buy another book, the two free books and gifts are mine to keep forever.

151 HDN EYS2 351 HDN EYTE

Name	(PLEASE PRINT)	
Address		Apt. #
City	State/Prov.	Zip/Postal Code

Signature (if under 18, a parent or guardian must sign)

Mail to the **Harlequin Reader Service:**
IN U.S.A.: P.O. Box 1867, Buffalo, NY 14240-1867
IN CANADA: P.O. Box 609, Fort Erie, Ontario L2A 5X3

Not valid to current subscribers of Harlequin Blaze books.

Want to try two free books from another line?
Call 1-800-873-8635 or visit www.morefreebooks.com.

* Terms and prices subject to change without notice. Prices do not include applicable taxes. N.Y. residents add applicable sales tax. Canadian residents will be charged applicable provincial taxes and GST. Offer not valid in Quebec. This offer is limited to one order per household. All orders subject to approval. Credit or debit balances in a customer's account(s) may be offset by any other outstanding balance owed by or to the customer. Please allow 4 to 6 weeks for delivery. Offer available while quantities last.

Your Privacy: Harlequin Books is committed to protecting your privacy. Our Privacy Policy is available online at www.eHarlequin.com or upon request from the Reader Service. From time to time we make our lists of customers available to reputable third parties who may have a product or service of interest to you. If you would prefer we not share your name and address, please check here. ☐

HB09R

You're invited to join our Tell Harlequin Reader Panel!

By joining our new reader panel you will:

- Receive Harlequin® books—they are FREE and yours to keep with no obligation to purchase anything!
- Participate in fun online surveys
- Exchange opinions and ideas with women just like you
- Have a say in our new book ideas and help us publish the best in women's fiction

In addition, you will have a chance to win great prizes and receive special gifts!
See Web site for details. Some conditions apply.
Space is limited.

To join, visit us at

www.TellHarlequin.com.

HARLEQUIN *Blaze*

COMING NEXT MONTH

Available September 29, 2009

#495 TOUCH ME Jacquie D'Alessandro
Historicals
After spending ten years as a nobleman's mistress, Genevieve Ralston's no stranger to good sex. So when she meets an irresistible stranger with seduction on his mind, she's game. Only little does she guess he wants much more than her body....

#496 CODY Kimberly Raye
Love at First Bite
All Miranda Rivers wants is a simple one-night stand. But when she picks up sexy rodeo star—and vampire—Cody Braddock, that one night might last an eternity....

#497 DANGEROUS CURVES Karen Anders
Undercover Lovers
Distract her rival agent, hot and handsome Max Carpenter, for two weeks—that's Rio Marshall's latest DEA assignment. But in the steamy Hawaiian hideaway, who'll be distracting whom?

#498 CAUGHT IN THE ACT Samantha Hunter
Dressed to Thrill
Wearing a bold 'n' sexy singer's costume has Gina Thomas delivering a standout performance that gives her the chance to search for scandalous photos of her sister. But it also captures the attention of Mason Scott—keeper of said photos. So what will he request when he catches Gina red-handed?

#499 RIPPED! Jennifer LaBrecque
Uniformly Hot!
Lieutenant Colonel Mitch Cooper is a play-by-the-rules kind of guy. Too bad his latest assignment is to keep an eye on free-spirited Eden Walters, who only wants to play...with him!

#500 SEDUCTION BY THE BOOK Stephanie Bond
Encounters
When four Southern wallflowers form a book club, they don't realize they're playing with fire. Because in *this* club, the members are reading classic erotic volumes, learning how to seduce the man of their dreams. After a book or two, Atlanta's male population won't stand a chance!

www.eHarlequin.com

HBCNMBPA0909